SOMETHING SUSPICIOUS IN SASKATCHEWAN

SOMETHING SUSPICIOUS IN SASKATCHEWAN

Dayle Campbell Gaetz

ORCA BOOK PUBLISHERS

Library and Archives Canada Cataloguing in Publication
Gaetz, Dayle, 1947-

Something suspicious in Saskatchewan / Dayle Campbell Gaetz.

ISBN 1-55143-565-9

I. Title.

PS8563.A25317S64 2006   jC813'.54   C2006-903480-X

First published in the United States, 2006
Library of Congress Control Number: 2006928998

Summary: Rusty and Katie uncover a sinister plot to run their aunt off the family farm.

Orca Book Publishers gratefully acknowledges the support for its publishing programs
provided by the following agencies: the Government of Canada through the Book Publishing
Industry Development Program and the Canada Council for the Arts, and the Province of
British Columbia through the BC Arts Council and the Book Publishing Tax Credit.

Cover design by Doug McCaffry
Cover illustration by Ljuba Levstek

Orca Book Publishers
PO Box 5626, Stn. B
Victoria, BC Canada
V8R 6S4

Orca Book Publishers
PO Box 468
Custer, WA USA
98240-0468

www.orcabook.com

Printed and bound in Canada

09 08 07 06 • 5 4 3 2 1

Other books in this mystery series by
Dayle Campbell Gaetz

Mystery from History
Barkerville Gold
Alberta Alibi

For Kristin K.,
a young and promising Saskatchewan writer.

Acknowledgments

To Harry, who owns a two thousand–acre farm in southern Saskatchewan, thanks for so patiently answering my many farm-related questions when we happened to sit next to you at Tim Hortons in Moose Jaw. And to Harry's assistant, originally from Neepawa, thanks for your input as well, and for suggesting we visit Margaret Laurence House in your home-town in Manitoba.

To "Gump" (Greg Gumpinger) at Moody's Equipment Ltd. in Unity, Saskatchewan, thanks for not laughing at an ignorant West Coaster's questions and for providing such excellent information about that amazing range of huge farm machinery.

To Andrew Wooldridge, thanks once again for your always valuable editing advice.

1

Katie pushed damp curls back from her forehead with hot sweaty fingers. She leaned sideways to peer past GJ's right ear. That straight dirt road still shot out in front of the truck as bland and boring as ever. It stretched endlessly across this dreary land until, in the distance, its two edges grew so close they seemed to touch.

On both sides of the road were fields. Rocky fields, bumpy fields, green fields, brown fields, they stretched in all directions to a flat and featureless horizon. In a place like this a truck might drive right off the edge of the earth and vanish forever. Worse than the flatness, though, was the heat. And dust. And mosquitoes.

"I hate Saskatchewan!" Katie announced.

Gram poked her head around the passenger seat. "We're almost at Aunt Margaret's farm." Her voice sounded dry and creaky as if she just woke up. "We'll all feel better when we get there."

"Not me. Not if Megan's there."

Gram's dark brown eyes fixed on Katie. "Katie, give Megan a break. The last time you saw your cousin she had just lost her father, so you can't blame her for being unhappy. Try being nice to her."

"I tried. It didn't work."

Two years ago, when Megan and Aunt Margaret had visited them in Victoria, nothing could please her older cousin. The girl complained about everything. Tall, swooping cedars in Katie's backyard? *Gloomy and depressing.* Snow-capped mountains in the distance? *Get in the way of the sky.* Sandy beaches teeming with life? *Ew—disgusting. It stinks worse than dead fish.*

"Why'd you come here if you hate everything so much?" Katie had shot back.

Megan's face had crumpled, and Katie felt bad. "I'm sorry. I didn't mean..."

"You're such a spoiled little brat! Just stay out of my face, and we'll get along fine."

"Besides," Gram continued now, "Megan was only fifteen then and going through a lot. I'm sure she's much more mature now that she's almost seventeen."

"Don't remind me," Katie groaned. "I really hate that I have to share my birthday with her."

"And I hate the way she treats me," Rusty added, "like I'm two years old."

"I'm sure you three cousins will have a wonderful time together," Gram said lamely. She must have tired of the conversation then because she flicked the radio on.

"Superweeds threaten to take over Saskatchewan," a man's voice announced.

Superweeds? Katie glanced out the window, half expecting to see a row of tree-sized weeds waving their hairy green leaves over the road, bending down, waiting to grab any unsuspecting truck that came along.

"Aren't you exaggerating?" a woman suggested.

"Not at all. These big biotech companies have unleashed a monster no one can control. They've genetically manipulated canola DNA and made new species that herbicides can't touch. The pollen blows through the air and contaminates other fields. Every year weeds become resistant to stronger herbicides. How do we farmers ever get rid of a superweed like that?"

"I guess that's for scientists to figure out," the woman said.

The man chuckled sadly. "Seems like they should have figured it out before they started pushing the seed at us."

"Thank you," the woman said. "We'll take more calls after the break."

Katie glanced at Rusty. He looked up from his sketchbook, a puzzled frown on his face.

"Here we are," GJ announced.

Beside the road was a marshy area filled with cattails. Then came a row of ordinary, leafy green trees—definitely not superweeds. Once past the trees Katie saw a white, two-story house set well back from the road. It had dark green trim and a steep green roof.

GJ slowed the truck to make the turn. Dragging its dusty white travel trailer, the truck barreled up the long driveway toward Aunt Margaret's house.

"What stinks?" Rusty wrinkled his nose. "It smells like a campfire after you dump water on it."

"Oh no!" Gram said. "It looks as if there's been a fire!"

"That's one way of killing weeds," GJ remarked.

"Revenge on the superweeds!" Rusty shouted.

Katie leaned toward the window on Rusty's side. A barbed wire fence ran alongside the driveway, and beyond it the wide lumpy field was black as soot. Scattered tendrils of gray smoke rose out of the charred ugliness and twisted into the still air. Fence posts beside the driveway were nothing more than blackened charred sticks held in place by long strands of barbed wire.

At the end of the driveway, across from the house, stood two white-planked sheds, about thirty feet apart. The remains of a third shed, closer to the field, may once have matched the other two. Now it was nothing more than a dirty cement foundation and a few charcoal-black posts pointing toward the endless blue sky.

Katie covered her nose against the acrid smell of smoke and wet ashes. She turned to look out the other side of the truck. On a square of dry brown grass in front of the farmhouse was a partly finished rock wall. Not far away stood a small stack of dusty gray rocks. Someone had made a feeble attempt at a garden in the dirt behind the rock wall, but nothing remained now except a forlorn little cluster of brown flowers that hung their heads in shame.

"Maybe the superweeds got them," Katie said, and Rusty laughed.

GJ blasted on the horn as they passed the burned-out shed. He honked again as he pulled to a stop across from the screened porch. Katie watched the back porch, waiting for the screen door to burst open. She pictured Aunt Margaret running down the three steps waving her arms, a huge smile lighting up her round face.

But nothing moved. The door didn't open; there was no sign of life.

"Maybe the superweeds got them," Rusty said.

Katie and Rusty both chuckled, but Gram ignored them. "Poor Margaret, she works so hard since Al died. She's likely out working in the fields." Gram shook her head. "I can't understand why she doesn't sell this place and move to Victoria."

Gram had been saying the same thing for two years now, ever since Uncle Al suffered a massive heart attack and died alone in the middle of a canola field.

"I wish they already had moved," Katie said. "Then we wouldn't have to be here."

Thin streaks of white cloud veiled the sunlight, but didn't lessen the heat. The truck grew hotter by the second. Still, the back door didn't open.

Despite the heat, a blur of mosquitoes swarmed around the truck as if daring the occupants to open a door.

"I hope they left the house unlocked," GJ said. "We can't stay here much longer or we'll roast."

"Maybe we should just leave," Katie suggested.

GJ honked the horn again, two impatient blasts.

The sound echoed back at them from somewhere on the driveway. Instinctively Katie swung around, only to be confronted by the blank, white front of her grandparents' travel trailer.

GJ looked in his side mirror. "There's a truck coming up the driveway."

"It must be Margaret," Gram's voice bubbled with excitement.

"Wait!" Katie cried. Too late. Both Gram and GJ flung their doors open and jumped out.

A wall of dry air slammed into the cab like a blast from a fiery oven. With it came a swirl of whining mosquitoes. Katie opened her door and slid to the ground. Puffs of dust fluttered between her bare toes, and her feet sizzled like chicken strips in a stir-fry. She ran to the back of the trailer and stopped in its narrow triangle of shade.

A black pickup truck had pulled to a stop behind the trailer, but it wasn't Aunt Margaret who stepped from the driver's side. It was a square-faced man, maybe thirty years old. He was shorter than GJ, at about five foot ten, and solidly built. He wore dusty jeans, a long-sleeved blue shirt and a gray baseball cap.

8

Gram made her way toward the passenger side with a cloud of mosquitoes around her head and GJ at her heels. She pulled open the door. Someone was sitting in the seat. A teenage girl with long, stringy blond hair and an ugly scowl. It had to be Megan. Or was it?

The girl stepped slowly out of the truck and turned to drag a bulging backpack from the seat. It bounced on the running board and thudded to the dirt beside her. She closed the door and turned to face Gram. Her lips parted and she showed her teeth. Katie wasn't sure if she was growling or grinning.

Gram looked the girl up and down and glanced back at GJ, her face crinkled with uncertainty.

No, Katie decided, this girl might look a little like Megan but was definitely not her cousin. Megan was a pretty girl, with shining blond hair, healthy glowing skin and a trim athletic build. This girl was way thin, like a stick figure, or a skeleton. Her long, skinny arms hung down like old bones from her black tank top and her elbows were sharp knobs in the middle. Even in this stifling heat she wore long black jeans, black socks and black sneakers. So how come Gram put her arms around this stranger and gave her a hug?

Katie moved closer to investigate.

Before she got there the man strode around the truck and slipped a protective arm across the girl's bony shoulders.

"Megan," he smiled at her, a wide friendly smile that made him look years younger. "Aren't you going to introduce me to your family?" His sky-blue eyes sparkled as he looked eagerly from Gram to GJ.

"Uh, yeah, I guess..." Megan didn't look at the man. She didn't look at anyone, but her eyes rolled around the farmyard in a confused way as if she were searching for something but couldn't remember what.

Katie tried not to stare. This was her cousin? This was Megan? It didn't seem possible. Katie realized she could have passed Megan on the street and not had a clue who she was. For one thing, Megan looked old. Like about twenty-four, or even older. And her eyes were so huge and so wide open they bugged out of her face like the eyes of a lizard.

Megan's cheekbones stuck out sharply above sunken cheeks. Her lips were dark purple like a bad bruise and, far from glowing, her pale skin resembled a bowl of oatmeal porridge. Dull.

The purple lips parted. "Uh, yeah," Megan repeated. "Cliff, this is my grandma and my grandpa Jerry from Victoria. Gram and GJ, Cliff."

"Welcome to Saskatchewan." Cliff smiled and stepped forward to shake hands first with Gram and then with GJ. Then he glanced uncertainly toward Katie and Rusty. He turned to Megan.

"Uh," Megan said, "and these are my uh, niece and nephew—er, no, they're my two little cousins, Kathryn and Russell."

Katie rolled her eyes at Rusty. His thin red eyebrows lifted and his blue eyes twinkled in his freckled face. With a wink at Katie, he grinned a wide cheesy grin and stepped forward.

"Well, I guess you must be old Clifford," he said. "Glad to meet you old man. Any friend of our ancient cousin Megan is a friend of ours." Rusty shook a surprised Cliff's hand. "You can call me Rusty if you like, everyone else does. And Megan's other little cousin over there likes to be called Katie."

Megan scowled.

"Where's your mother?" Gram asked.

Megan glanced at her watch. "Must be in the kitchen."

"We honked and no one came to the door," GJ told her.

Megan's eyes flicked toward Cliff and away. Two creases appeared between her eyebrows. "Said she'd be back before four—wanted to be home when you arrived." Megan started toward the house, dragging her backpack across the dusty driveway. She stopped on the small outside porch to kick off her shoes. Seconds later the screen door slammed behind her.

"Margaret must have the radio on," Cliff tried to reassure Gram. "She wouldn't have heard you."

The door swung open again. "She's not here!" Megan called. She slipped her bare feet into a pair of shiny pink flip-flops.

Cliff ran toward the truck. "I told her not to finish haying that field by herself! The windrower keeps breaking down."

"If you're going to look for her I'm coming too," Gram scrambled into the passenger seat, and GJ squeezed in beside her.

By the time Cliff started the engine Katie and Rusty had climbed over the tailgate into the truck box and settled with their backs against the cab. Megan remained near the porch, her long, thin arms crossed over her sunken chest. She watched them go, bouncing toward the nearest field. Suddenly the truck skidded to a stop and backed up in a swirl of dust.

"Hop in!" Cliff called. "We might need you."

"Yeah? What for?" Megan stepped back.

"Megan, please, just get in," Cliff pleaded.

Megan glanced from Cliff, to the house, to the truck box. Then her shoulders slumped and she climbed in obediently. She sat down, her arms behind her, draped awkwardly over the tailgate. Her wide, watery blue eyes stared straight at Katie.

Katie squirmed uncomfortably. She tried to avoid Megan's eyes. But when Megan continued to stare, Katie decided to stare right back. That's when she realized her cousin wasn't seeing her at all. Megan's eyes were blank and empty, looking at absolutely nothing.

Katie turned to Rusty, a question in her eyes. He shook his head sadly.

2

Aunt Margaret was not hard to find. How could anything be hard to find on this land where you can see forever? Katie twisted around and leaned over the truck's side to see where they were going. Wind blew hot and dry in her face, and the wide truck tires stirred up clouds of dust. She squinted into the distance, her eyes streamed gritty tears.

Beyond a bright green field and a sunshine yellow one, a tall red tractor perched high above a sea of golden grass. Cliff drove straight toward it.

They rode alongside a slough filled with brown and broken stalks of cattails. Dozens of red-winged black-birds perched on the stalks like tiny sentinels with scar-let patches on their shoulders. Standing in the murky water was a post that supported an object the size of a rural mailbox. Its thick cylindrical walls were made of tightly woven straw. The inside looked hollow.

Katie wondered what it was. She turned to ask Megan, but one glance at her cousin's blank stare and she changed her mind.

The truck bumped to a stop near the tractor, and Katie clambered over the side. She landed in tall golden grass. Or maybe it was hay—yes, this must be the hay field Cliff mentioned.

The truck doors flew open and all three adults ran toward the tractor. Katie followed more slowly, stepping lightly on hay that grew sharp and prickly under her bare feet. The tractor was one of those weird-looking ones she had seen lined up for sale in every little town they had passed through since leaving Alberta's ranchland. Its big back tires had heavy tread like a normal tractor, but the front ones were small and smooth. They were attached to the frame by two weird arm-like projections that bent at the middle like elbows. The machine perched above the hay field like a huge, mechanical grasshopper.

When she reached the side of the tractor and looked up at the cab, Katie realized her mistake. The small wheels were actually at the back of the machine. In front of the big tractor tires was a wide attachment that resembled an over-sized lawn mower blade, the kind used to cut the grass in parks back home. Printed in neat white letters on it were two words: *Harvest Header*.

"Margaret!" Gram dropped to her knees.

Katie crouched beside her. Just visible beneath the tractor was a pair of brown leather boots.

"Mom?" a metallic voice echoed from underneath.

"Margaret." GJ put his hand on the red metal side and bent to peer underneath. "Are you all right?"

"Yes," the voice hesitated, "but I'm sort of stuck."

On her knees, Katie crept closer. Attached to the boots, a pair of jean-clad legs lay on top of hay stubble between the two high front wheels. Not much else showed of Aunt Margaret other than a scrap of green plaid shirt. Her arms were lost somewhere up under the header.

"Is your arm caught?" GJ called.

"No, Dad, don't worry. The sleeve of my shirt got hung up under the cutter bar. It's all tangled in there, and I can't pull it loose."

"We need a couple of jacks," Cliff sounded agitated. "We'll have to lift the windrower."

Katie turned and squinted up at him. His face was black against the bright sun behind him. "What's a windrower?"

Cliff shifted his weight from one leg to the other and didn't seem to hear Katie. But Megan, who was leaning against the truck bumper hugging her arms around her bony body, rolled her eyes impressively. She stepped quickly out of the way when Cliff started toward the truck at a run.

"I'm going to get a jack, some rope, and..."

"Why don't I just wriggle under and cut her sleeve loose?" Katie asked.

But no one answered; they were too busy worrying about Aunt Margaret and making hasty plans.

"I'll go with you." GJ hurried toward Cliff. "I've got a good jack in my truck, and we'll need some blocks. I think..."

Gram jumped up. "Katie's right!" she shouted, her voice loud in the still air.

Both men stopped as if they had slammed into an invisible wall. They swung around, mouths open in identical, round circles of surprise.

"There's room for someone small like Katie to squirm under and cut Margaret's sleeve free. If you're going to do any jacking up, you'd better wait until my daughter is out of there!"

Cliff rubbed his hand over his whiskers and glanced at GJ, who nodded agreement. "It's worth a try," he said.

"I don't suppose anyone has a pair of scissors?" Gram asked.

For a silent moment everyone looked at everyone else. Then Rusty said, "Here, take my Swiss Army knife." He pulled the closed knife from his shorts' pocket and handed it to Katie.

"Be careful, Katie," Gram said.

Katie lay down on the sharp remains of cut hay. It felt like a thousand sharp sticks poking into her back as she wormed her way between the big wheels and wriggled up close toward the header beside her aunt. A horde of mosquitoes must have been hiding in the hay, because suddenly they were everywhere, landing on her face and bare arms and legs. She did her best to ignore them. "Hi, Aunt Margaret," Katie said to the plaid-clad shoulder. "I bet you were glad to hear us coming."

"You're not kidding! If I had to lie here much longer I'd be nothing but one massive mosquito bite."

"So, do you do this sort of thing often around here?"

Aunt Margaret laughed. "Only when I'm expecting company. It's my way of avoiding cooking."

"Well, I hate to break the bad news, but all this rescuing is gonna give everyone a huge appetite."

Aunt Margaret made an odd sound in her throat and muttered something about Megan.

"Which sleeve is caught?" Katie asked.

"The left one, closest to you. If you can wriggle just a little farther forward you should be able to reach up and cut it loose."

Katie opened the knife and, holding it in one hand with her arms over her head, inched forward using her heels and bent knees. Her right hand found Aunt Margaret's left arm and she wrapped her fingers in the cotton shirt fabric.

"Just cut the sleeve right off at my elbow," Aunt Margaret said. "You'll never free it from the cutter bar."

"Okay, but don't forget to tell me if I slice into your arm."

"Don't worry, you'll hear me loud and clear."

It wasn't as easy as it sounded. Katie bunched up the cotton and struggled to work the knife tip through. But there wasn't much room to move and she couldn't see what she was doing in this confined space with her arms stretched above her head. The knife tip refused to break through the fabric. Katie held her breath. What if the knife slipped? What if she stabbed Aunt Margaret's arm? She could slice into an artery, blood would spurt everywhere.

Katie was suddenly way too hot, her face damp with sweat. A frightened little squeak slipped from her throat.

"Katie," Aunt Margaret said calmly. "Take a deep breath. Don't worry, you can do this, you won't cut me. Besides I'm a tough old bird."

Katie took her aunt's advice. She paused, took a long deep breath, let it out, and tried again. One quick slice and the knife slipped through the shirt-sleeve. After that she sliced and hacked, holding the material away from her aunt's arm as she worked her way around the sleeve. Mosquitoes whined in her ears and tickled her face with their landings. But there was nothing she could do about them, except work a little faster.

At last the sleeve came free. "Ahh." Aunt Margaret pulled her arm to her side. "Let's get out of here!"

The minute they were both standing up, free of the windrower, Aunt Margaret engulfed Katie in a grateful hug. "Thanks for rescuing me."

"Anytime," Katie said, pulling away. "But what happened?"

"It's the strangest thing." A confused look came over Aunt Margaret's face. Confusion and something else. Worry? She glanced in Megan's direction and then back to Katie. "It seems a piece of chicken wire got left in the field. It was hidden in the hay, and I didn't spot it until too late. I was trying to free it from around the cutter bar when my sleeve got caught up."

"Oh, Margaret, you had us so worried." Gram stepped up to wrap her arms around Aunt Margaret.

She placed her hands on Margaret's shoulders and took a half step back to study her daughter's face. "But I don't understand how wire could get left out here. I'd think you would all be very careful about things like that."

"I don't know, Mom." Again she glanced over at Megan, who stared back at her, unflinching. "I can't imagine anyone here being so careless. That harvest header is an expensive piece of equipment, and we can't afford to damage it."

"Just say it why don't you?" Megan's shout made everyone jump.

Megan looked at Gram. "My mother thinks it's my fault." She swung around and stomped away, parting the hay in front of her as she went.

"I don't understand." Gram turned to Aunt Margaret.

Aunt Margaret bit her lip. "Let's talk about it later, Mom."

Cliff walked to the front of the header and crouched low for a closer look. "It's chicken wire all right," he said, getting to his feet. "But it can't be Megan's fault. I warned you we hadn't seen the last of Scott."

"Who's Scott?" Katie asked.

3

Cliff pulled off his baseball cap and ran his fingers through straight sand-colored hair that flopped lazily over a forehead beaded with sweat. His blue eyes swept past Katie and sought out Aunt Margaret.

Why didn't he answer her? Why did he study Aunt Margaret as if asking permission to continue?

"Who-is-Scott?" Katie repeated.

Cliff stuck his cap back on and pulled it low on his forehead. His face was flushed from heat that hung over the field like a thick quilt. Slowly his eyes moved to Katie. "Scott used to help out around here, but we had to let him go."

"Why?"

Cliff hesitated. Again his eyes glanced over to Aunt Margaret. She nodded, almost imperceptibly.

Cliff's gaze shifted to the ground where he studied

the toe of his workboot. When he answered, it was in a half-whisper, as if he hated to speak badly of anyone. "Your aunt caught him stealing."

Finally Aunt Margaret spoke up. "Scott's a young fellow, who just graduated from high school," she said. "I hired him to help out with the seeding in June." She glanced over Katie's shoulder. Frown lines appeared on her forehead and her lips tightened. "He seemed like a nice enough boy. I couldn't believe he would steal from us."

Katie turned to see what her aunt was looking at. Thin as a fence post and topped by a tangle of hair that blended perfectly with the hay, Megan stepped carefully in her pink flip-flops, following the path of flattened hay made by the truck tires. Her bone-thin arms flapped uselessly at her sides like two broken wings.

Cliff also watched Megan's progress toward the farmhouse. "I never trusted that boy," he said quietly. "And now I catch him hanging around the farm at all hours of the day and night. I swear he's trying to get even."

"With who? For what?" Katie paused. When Cliff didn't reply she asked, "Do you think he sneaked into the hay field and left that hunk of wire because you fired him? What good would that do him?"

"None at all," Aunt Margaret said. "I'm sure it was just an accident, nothing to do with Scott."

"Yeah, and I guess the fire that burned down the feed shed two days ago wasn't his fault either?" asked Cliff.

"It was an accident," Aunt Margaret insisted. "Megan burned off the flax straw, the fire wasn't quite out, and the wind did the rest."

"I told you I saw...," Cliff started, but Aunt Margaret cut him off.

"Let's all hop in the truck and head for the house. I don't know about all of you, but I'm thirsty enough to drink a gallon of water and I need to think about getting dinner ready."

Cliff drove so fast, bumping over the uneven field, that Katie had to hold on tight to the side of the truck box. Bouncing along, she managed to lean over the side and face forward, into the wind, where Megan still walked in the track.

The truck raced closer and closer, as if Cliff would run Megan down. Couldn't she hear? Why didn't she step out of the way? Why didn't Cliff slow down? It was like a game of chicken. And Cliff was the one to give in. He slowed and pulled around Megan to stop beside her. He leaned out the driver's side window with a friendly smile. "Hey, lady," he said, "want a ride?"

Megan turned and stood uncertainly, looking at all the faces that looked back at her. Cliff, Gram and GJ from inside the cab. Katie, Rusty and her own mother from the box behind. Without bothering to reply, Megan stepped onto the back bumper and swung over the tailgate into the truck box where she settled in the opposite corner to her mother. Aunt Margaret leaned forward to pat her daughter's bent knee.

Megan retreated further into the corner. She stared across the fields toward the distant line of the horizon. The truck started up again, more slowly this time.

Fifteen minutes later they were all gathered around a long rectangular table in the old-fashioned farmhouse kitchen, a tall frosty glass of ice-cold lemonade in front of each person. Except Megan. The teenager leaned against the sink, clutching a glass of water and studying the purple toenails that peeked out from beneath her black jeans.

In the center of the table was a bowl of taco chips along with salsa and sour cream that Gram had brought in from the trailer. Rusty and Cliff seemed involved in a serious competition to see who could eat the most in the shortest period of time.

Katie half-listened to Gram, GJ and Aunt Margaret chat while she crunched into a salty taco chip with a scoop of tomatoey salsa and cool sour cream. A hot spicy aftertaste burned her tongue, and she reached for her lemonade.

"I'm putting Katie upstairs with Megan. I'm sure these two girls have a lot in common now that Katie is getting so grown up."

Katie choked on her lemonade.

"Good idea," Gram agreed.

Katie's glass slammed so hard on the table a slop of watery-yellow liquid sloshed over the top. She watched it trickle down the side. "Um...I'd rather sleep in the trailer." Her voice came out angry, with a high-pitched edge of panic. How could they do this to her?

Time stopped. Everyone froze. Every eye stared at her. Katie fumbled for words.

Megan saved the day. "Oh, Moth-er!" she drawled. "You have got to be kidding!"

Still clutching the water glass, she folded her arms across her non-existent stomach. "What's wrong with the trailer?"

"Exactly," Katie said.

"Nothing's wrong with it," Gram said. "Except that it will be stifling hot out there, and we don't want to waste electricity by plugging into Aunt Margaret's power for our air-conditioning unit. Why should we when there's a huge, perfectly good house right here, with four bedrooms upstairs?"

You think those bedrooms won't be stifling hot? Katie wanted to say, but Gram hadn't finished yet. She fixed Katie with a firm, uncompromising glare.

"Besides, your aunt has gone to the trouble of preparing a bed for you with lovely, crisp, fresh sheets. Won't that be nice after using a sleeping bag for so long? And I can get all our bedding washed while we're here."

Katie knew what was expected of her. She was supposed to quit complaining and start acting grateful. But she wasn't grateful. As if simply being here wasn't bad enough, now she had to share a room with Megan? Couldn't anyone else see how Megan scowled at her, as if all of this was Katie's fault? Katie shuddered and opened her mouth to object.

This time GJ headed her off. "Katie is speechless with joy," he said. "Thanks, Margaret, I'm sure these two cousins will become great friends in no time."

No time is right, Katie thought. No time, no way, not never.

"She's speechless with something," Rusty commented before stuffing a handful of chips into his mouth. He chewed thoughtfully, swallowed and grinned at Katie. "I think it's great! You and Megan will get to bond!"

Before Katie could reply he added, "And I can hardly wait to sleep in a real bed tonight. In a room to myself! You have to admit, Katie, those bunks in the trailer aren't the most comfortable beds in the world. Weren't you complaining about yours just a few nights ago?"

Katie glared at her younger cousin. If he were close enough, she'd kick him in the shins, under the table where no one would see. Rusty grinned again, as if he knew exactly what she was thinking. Then he pulled the biggest taco chip out of the pile, scooped up a whopping load of salsa and sour cream and opened his mouth wide to shove the whole mess in at once.

While Gram and Aunt Margaret, with reluctant help from Megan, set about making dinner, Cliff and GJ decided to head back out to the windrower.

"We need to jack it up so I can get underneath and cut that wire away from the cutter bar," Cliff said, pushing up from the table.

"I'll get that extra jack from my truck," GJ offered as they headed for the door.

"Hey, yeah, okay. See you in a sec, I need to grab some wire cutters from the equipment shed."

The screen door slammed behind them, but Katie watched them through a window of the screened porch. Cliff disappeared to the left. GJ moved to the right, toward his truck. Katie picked up a taco chip and bit into it.

"Ready?" She heard GJ call.

Cliff walked past, shoving a red-handled tool into his back pocket. A truck engine roared to life. Wheels crunched over dirt and gravel. Katie jumped to her feet. "I'm going out to get my stuff from the trailer," she announced, glancing at Rusty. "Want to come?"

"Uh-uh." Rusty's hand hovered over the taco chips. "I'm busy."

Katie wrinkled her brow. She shifted her gaze to the door and quickly back to Rusty. She needed to talk to him. Outside. Now.

Rusty got the message. He grabbed a handful of chips, pushed back his chair and got to his feet. "Why not?" he said. "The sooner I get settled in my own room the better."

Katie pushed the screen door open with both hands and hurried outside. Hot dry air slapped her in the face, the acrid stink of burned straw filled her nostrils, and a swarm of mosquitoes dive-bombed in for the kill. She turned left and started across the driveway at a run.

"Hey, where are you going?" Rusty ran after her.

4

Katie studied the shed in front of her. Roughly the size of a one-car garage, it was built of wide vertical planks painted white.

Rusty stopped beside her. "What's up?"

"We need to check out the equipment shed."

"Who says this is the equipment shed?"

"Me."

"As if you know."

Katie rolled her eyes. "I saw Cliff turn this way." She nodded toward the other, almost identical shed, more than thirty feet away. "And he didn't have time to go to that one and back."

She pulled the door open. It creaked on rusty hinges as Katie stepped from dazzling sunlight into the shed's dim light.

Rusty stopped in the doorway. "What are we looking for?"

"Can't you guess?"

"Not a clue."

"Actually, that's exactly what we're here for."

"What? A clue? To what?"

"To who left that wire out in the field. I can't believe it was an accident, because who would be so stupid?"

"Oh, I don't know...Megan comes to mind. That girl is totally out of it."

"Cliff thinks it was Scott."

Rusty shrugged. "Yeah, but I can't figure out why. I mean, if Scott did it, it wasn't a mistake. But why go to all the bother?" He shook his head. "I'm sure it was Megan, and she just forgot to pick it up."

"But why would Megan have wire out in the hay field? Why would anyone?"

As Katie's eyes adjusted to the light, she saw rows of tools hung neatly against the walls, each on its own bracket. Bigger items like shovels, hoes and pitchforks hung on lower brackets while smaller tools such as trowels and pruners were arranged above. Printed neatly in black felt pen above each tool was its correct name. There was one empty bracket: "Wire Cutters."

On the floor at the far end of the shed stood a large coil of barbed wire, fastened neatly so it wouldn't come undone. A smaller coil of chicken wire lay crookedly on a wide shelf above, its loose end stuck out in sharp jagged spikes beyond the shelf edge.

"Look at that," she whispered.

"Wow! Wire! In an equipment shed!" Rusty said. "On a farm! Will wonders never cease?"

"Don't be a dope, Rusty. Can't you see it's the only thing that's not properly put away? As if the last person to cut wire off the coil wasn't the usual, freakishly tidy person who normally uses this shed?"

"Or someone who was in a hurry?"

"Exactly. Someone who didn't want to get caught."

"Caught at what? Being messy? I may be wrong, but I don't think messiness is a crime, even in such a neat province as Saskatchewan."

"Well, but look how the wire is cut, it's all crooked and jagged." She ran her fingers over the thin wire mesh. "And this is the same kind of wire that jammed the cutter bar, I'm sure of it."

"So?"

"So..." Katie glanced at Rusty. He stared back as if she had lost her mind. Her shoulders slumped. Rusty was right. Someone cut a piece of chicken wire crookedly from a coil and didn't put the coil back as neatly as it should be. Big deal.

Nevertheless, if whoever cut the wire was in a big hurry, maybe Cliff was right. Maybe it was Scott and he didn't want to be seen. Or, maybe it was Megan and she didn't care. Katie could prove nothing.

"Let's go." Rusty stepped outside. "We're wasting our time here."

Katie sighed and followed her cousin. They darted along the driveway through a living whining blizzard of mosquitoes, more now that the heat of day had lessened. At the trailer they dashed inside and slammed the door. "Why does anyone want to live in this place?" Rusty asked.

"Who knows? Maybe it grows on you."

Katie's bunk was the bottom one at the back of the trailer. The top one had been Sheila's, but Rusty took over after Sheila's defection. Katie pulled open the drawer beneath her bunk, scooped up all the clothes she might need and stuffed them into her backpack. She slid her notebook from under the mattress and flipped it open. Grabbing the pen tucked inside she wrote.

Suspicious goings-on:
fire—how did it start?
Aunt Margaret's accident—was it sabotage?
Cliff sees Scott around the farm
Aunt Margaret fired Scott for stealing—what?
Jagged chicken wire—is it a clue?

When she had more time she would fill in the details. Now she slung her pack over her shoulder and started for the door. "I'm getting my mystery novel from the truck."

Rusty jammed a pair of jeans into his backpack. "Wait for me. I need my sketchbook."

A few minutes later, following her aunt's instructions, Katie reached the top stair and swung around to her left. She took a deep breath and started down a hallway lit only by a small rectangular window at one end.

Second door, right side, she reminded herself. She paused in front of a heavy wooden door. It was open an inch. Should she knock? Her arms were filled with her backpack, notebook and novel, so she decided to call Megan's name instead. But then she heard Megan mumble something that might have been "Come on in."

Katie took a quick breath and pushed the door open with her foot.

"Haven't you heard about knocking?" Megan snapped. On the floor near her bed she paused in the midst of a sit-up, legs bent, spine curled forward. She pulled something away from the far side of her face, something small, held in one hand. At the same moment there was a faint beep.

Katie stopped in the doorway. "What was that? Was that you? Have you got a cell phone? Do you always do sit-ups when you're on the phone?"

"If you don't exercise you get fat." Megan looked Katie up and down. "You should know that." She did two more sit-ups. Her backpack lay deflated on the floor. Clothing was scattered over her bed. Black jeans, black shirts, a black leather jacket and a pile of underwear. All black.

"Have you been away?"

Megan scrambled to her feet. "None of your business. What are you, the question police?"

Katie swallowed. Wasn't this going to be fun? She and her cousin, bonding? Okay, maybe she didn't start things off exactly right. She made a mental note not to ask any more questions. "Don't tell me, let me guess what your favorite color is." She tried to laugh. It sounded like a hiccup.

Megan's blue eyes blazed with quick fiery anger. Katie choked on her next word. It was meant to be *black*. "Bu-uu," she said. Like a burp.

Megan shook her head sadly, turned away and scooped up an armload of clothes. She stormed over to her dresser where she balanced on one foot, tried to hook her bare toes under a drawer handle and stumbled back.

"Want me to open it for you?" Katie asked, dumping her own stuff on the floor. Oops—did that count as a question?

Megan growled.

"I'm going to assume that means yes," Katie said. She walked boldly over, slid open the drawer and stepped quickly out of the way. Megan dropped all the clothes inside, spread them out and squashed them down until she could close the drawer.

"Thanks," she mumbled.

"No problem." Katie glanced around the room. Megan's bed was near the one small rectangular window, closed up tight. Its shade was up and sunlight streamed in. Already Katie was covered in a fine layer of perspiration, and she wondered how Megan, still wearing her black jeans, could stand this heat.

Pushed up against the wall on the far side of the room was a small folding cot with yellow flowered sheets, a matching pillow and a light creamy blanket. "I guess that's for me," Katie observed.

"Whatever," Megan mumbled. She flopped on her bed and picked up a book.

Katie squinted at the front cover, stepped closer, and was surprised to see it was an Agatha Christie novel. "So, do you like mysteries?"

"Question," Megan growled and pulled the book closer to her face.

Katie swallowed. "Oh, yeah, sorry." She resolved to keep quiet, to not say another word. So she was taken by surprise when the words slipped out anyway. "Hey, Megan, thanks for sharing your room. I bet we're going to have fun." Her words hung in the air like icicles.

Megan's cold blue eyes glared over the top of her book. "Do you even know how to stop talking?"

A chill ran down the back of Katie's neck. She picked up her stuff and dumped it on the cot. She grabbed her novel, notebook and pen, and left the room. That was enough bonding for one day.

5

Katie padded barefoot down the steep wooden staircase. She had almost reached the bottom when she became aware of quiet voices in the kitchen below. She paused. Although they were barely above a whisper, Katie recognized Gram's, GJ's and Aunt Margaret's voices. She waited, listening, thought she heard the word "airport," but couldn't be sure, so crept down one more stair. It creaked beneath her foot.

The voices stopped. Katie continued down the stairs. "What's going on?" she asked, surprised to see Rusty seated at the table too.

No one seemed inclined to answer, and when the phone rang Aunt Margaret flew out of her chair as if she'd been stung. "I'll get it in my office," she said, giving Katie a nervous glance on her way past.

From her position, Katie could see into the tiny office tucked behind the kitchen, a room that had

once been the pantry. Aunt Margaret ran to the desk
and stopped abruptly. She hesitated, her hand hover-
ing over the phone. It rang again, and she snapped
it up.

"Yes?" she whispered.

She listened, then pressed a hand to her forehead.
"Who is this?"

Intrigued, Katie stepped closer.

"Katie, come on in and join us," GJ called. "Let
your aunt talk on the phone in peace."

"But..." Katie glanced at GJ and back to Aunt
Margaret, who was working her way around her desk
to the chair. She sank into it, white-faced, the phone
clutched tight against her ear.

"Katie, don't be so rude." Gram's chair scraped
across the floor as she stood up.

Katie hesitated. Something was wrong. She knew
it. Deep inside herself she knew it. She could never
understand why, but she always got this same strange
feeling, a sense of curiosity, a need to delve deeper,
when there was a crime being conceived, a mystery
in the making. Even if Rusty and Sheila made fun of
her when she tried to explain, she always knew.

But what could she say? The main reason her
grandparents had brought her and Rusty and Sheila
along on this trip was to keep the three of them out

of trouble for the summer. No mysteries allowed. No getting into trouble, no causing worries for Gram and GJ. They had all promised. Even if Sheila had deserted them, the promise still held.

Aunt Margaret replaced the receiver and buried her face in her hands.

"Katie?" Gram walked toward her, looking bewildered.

"Sorry, I felt a little weird for a minute there. Dizzy. I guess I must be hungry." She rubbed her stomach.

Gram took her by the arm and led her to the table. "Dinner is ready. We'll eat just as soon as your aunt is finished on the phone."

Minutes later Aunt Margaret emerged from her office. She attempted a smile but her lips trembled and she turned away. Katie glanced at Gram to see if she noticed it too, but her grandmother was busy at the stove.

Aunt Margaret stopped at the bottom of the stairs. "Megan!" she called, and waited. "Dinner!" When there was no answer, Aunt Margaret went to help Gram dish up the food.

Fried chicken, potato salad, green salad and fresh bakery bread was piled on the table, and everyone dug in. The adults chatted and laughed about the good old days when Aunt Margaret, Katie's mom and Rusty's mom were kids.

"Where's Cliff?" Rusty asked when there was a lull in the conversation. "Doesn't he live here too?"

"Not exactly. He usually has breakfast with us because he starts work so early, but he has his own kitchen," Aunt Margaret explained. "This house was built for a big family, and we didn't need all the space, so years ago your Uncle Al and I converted some of the back rooms into a separate suite. Cliff seems happy there."

Katie studied Aunt Margaret. For the third time her aunt's eyes slid over to the clock on the microwave then to the wall phone. She took a small bite of potato salad. When the phone rang, her fork fell from her hand. It bounced off her plate and clattered onto the floor. She didn't seem to notice. She leaned forward as if to get up, but then changed her mind and sat very still, her fingers on the table edge.

The phone rang again. She cringed.

GJ, sitting beside Aunt Margaret, bent to pick up her fork. "Maybe you should answer your phone," he suggested.

"No!" she snapped.

GJ's jaw fell.

"Oh, Dad, I'm sorry." Aunt Margaret placed a hand on his arm just as the phone rang for the third time. "It will be someone trying to sell me something. They always phone at dinnertime."

On the fourth ring, the answering machine in the office picked up. Two seconds later there was a rumble on the stairs, and a second after that Megan burst into the room. "Why didn't you answer the phone?" she demanded.

"I'm tired of telemarketers," her mother said. "I already got one call this evening, and there are usually at least two or three."

"But it might be important!" Megan screeched.

Aunt Margaret remained calm. "If it is, they'll leave a message." She hesitated, then added, "I'm not sure why you're so worried, honey. Your friends always call on your cell phone anyway."

Megan swung around and stormed into Aunt Margaret's office. In a flash she was back. "No messages!" she shouted and strode to the sink. She grabbed a glass, filled it with water and turned to glare at her mother. "That stinks!" she said.

"You're not kidding," Rusty said. "What's wrong with the water around here anyway? It tastes like mud."

Megan rolled her eyes. "I'm not talking about the water. Doesn't anyone listen to me? I'm talking about the phone. It stinks that my mother doesn't bother to answer it anymore."

The room grew so quiet they could hear mosquitoes beating at the window. Aunt Margaret stared speechlessly at her daughter. Gram pressed her lips together and looked at GJ who frowned back, shaking his head. Katie's eyes flicked from one to the other around the kitchen. Rusty bit into a chicken leg.

"Megan...," Aunt Margaret began.

Megan's thin body slumped against the counter. "I'm sorry, Mom. It's just...I feel so...I don't feel so good."

You don't look so good either, Katie almost said, but the tension in this room was too strong. She couldn't force herself to speak.

"You're probably hungry," GJ said. "You look as if you haven't eaten in a month."

"Come, sit by me." Gram smiled invitingly and patted the empty chair. "Have something to eat."

To Katie's surprise, Megan nodded. She sat down and piled green salad onto her plate. When Megan started to eat, Gram slipped a piece of chicken next to the salad and followed it with a thick slice of multigrain bread. Megan didn't object. She nibbled on the chicken, ripped the bread in two and swallowed a few of the crumbs, then returned to her salad.

All the excited chatter between Gram, Aunt Margaret and GJ had ended with the arrival of

Megan. Now, in the uneasy silence, the sounds of chewing and swallowing seemed to bounce off the walls. Katie could hardly wait to get away. She needed to find a quiet place to sit and fill out her notebook.

Half an hour dragged by before Katie, clutching her notebook and a tall glass of water, escaped to a white wicker chair on the screened porch. She was so thirsty she drank most of the water right away, and then she placed the glass on the small wicker table beside her.

Although the sun still beat down mercilessly on the flat dry prairie, it had dipped lower in that great huge sky. The porch was deep in shade, but the evening air hung hot and thick around her. Not a breath of wind stirred across the dusty driveway, not a whisper through the screened windows.

The house cast its long shadow over the driveway, its gabled roof pointed at the burnt-out field like a fat arrowhead. To Katie's right, the travel trailer, GJ's silver truck and the black farm truck were all in shade. A movement to her left caught her eye.

A long shadow, the shape of a man's head and shoulders, moved across the dirt, growing steadily bigger until Cliff himself appeared around the corner of the house. Dressed in clean jeans and a white cotton shirt, he crossed in front of her and climbed into the black truck. A minute later, he headed down the driveway followed by a trail of dust.

Katie opened her notebook and scanned the notes she had jotted down earlier about the fire, the accident, and so on. Right now she couldn't think of anything to add, so she flipped to a clean page.

She wrote *Saskatchewan* in big letters across the top. Then she sat quite still, staring straight ahead at minute squares of thread-thin screening, at puffs of dust that filtered through, at mosquitoes that bounced off the screen. Finally she looked down at her notebook and started to write, pausing often to tap her pen against her chin.

Chicken wire in the hay field—what's that about?
Sabotage? Could be Scott—need to meet him.
Carelessness? Who else but Megan? She has recently misplaced her brain.
A freak accident? Cliff or Aunt Margaret—overworked & underpaid.
Speaking of "freak," what about that Megan? Why'd she freak-out when I went into her room?

*She knew I was coming, didn't she? Why were
all those clothes piled on her bed? Did they come
from her backpack? Maybe she was going somewhere and changed her mind. Maybe she just got
back from somewhere. Maybe she was running
away. Why?*

*Does Megan even know what she's doing? She
looks like a walking skeleton—does she seriously
think she's fat?*

*Something's bugging Aunt Margaret—some-
thing or someone. That was no telemarketer
who phoned tonight. A.M. was scared.*

How do I know?

*She acted nervous even before she answered
the phone. That means she's had calls before.
Probably lots of them at the same time of day,
that's why she didn't answer when the phone
rang later.*

So:

Is someone threatening her?

*Who? Scott? Possible, don't know, need to
meet him. NOTE: Cliff would say it's Scott, if he
knew about the calls. Does he?*

*Megan? Maybe, who knows? NOTE: Megan
could have used her cell phone—Hey! Maybe
that's why she freaked-out when I walked into*

her room, maybe I interrupted her in the middle of a threatening phone call.

Problems with Megan theory:

Wouldn't A.M. recognize her own daughter's voice?

Maybe not, if Megan whispered. Maybe that's why Megan freaked-out again when A.M. didn't answer the phone, because, how do you make a threatening phone call if no one answers?

Why would Megan threaten her own mother?

Don't know, maybe Rusty's right, maybe she's out of her mind.

Either that or she's trying to tell her mother something.

I figure it has to be a revenge thing (Scott), or an out-of-her-mind thing (Megan), because A.M. doesn't have anything worth threatening about, like money. GJ says farmland isn't worth a whole lot these days, so I guess she's stuck here for the rest of her life. Megan too.

Ugh! No wonder she's depressed.

I'm depressed too. That's because I don't know anything. I haven't found one real clue.

Now that I think about it, I haven't found a real crime either.

Bummer.

This is to going to be the longest, boringest, hottest, buggiest week of my entire life. I feel like I've been here a week already, and this is only the first day! How will I ever survive? I wish Sheila was here.

No, scratch that. I'm never speaking to Sheila again as long as I live.

I mean, I went to all that trouble to save her dad's skin—not to mention his ranch—and what does Sheila do? Stays behind with him! Even when she knew I need her here.

How could she do this to me?

"Whatcha doin'?"

Katie jumped at the sound of Rusty's voice. He flopped down on the wicker loveseat and leaned back on its pillows.

"Nothing." She flipped her notebook shut.

"Oh. Because I thought, maybe you were writing notes."

Katie shrugged.

"But," Rusty went on, "since you're not, I guess you don't care what I found out."

Katie curled her fingers around the top of her notebook. She stared down at them. Eight round little fingernails, like pale white faces looking up at her. Curious.

Rusty started to hum. From the corner of her eye she saw him sit up and open his sketchbook. He bent over it, a pencil in his hand.

She did not want to ask. She tried not to ask. She had to ask. "Okay, what did you find out?"

When Rusty kept on drawing as if he hadn't heard, she leaned over to see. Big round eyes looked up at her from a long triangular face. "What's that? A cow?"

Rusty looked smug, as if he knew something she didn't. "You know the accident with the wind-rower?"

"Of course," she snapped. "I was there, remember?"

Rusty shrugged and returned to his sketching.

"Okay, Rusty, I'm sorry. Yes, I know the accident. What about it?"

"That wasn't the first."

"Wire got caught in the cutter bar before?"

Rusty shook his head impatiently. "No, but Aunt Margaret said that last week the stock got out—"

"Stock? What stock? Got out of what?"

"Stock. Farm animals, you know—"

"You mean cows? Is that why you're drawing a cow?"

"Yeah, okay, cows. Some of them escaped from the pasture last week. They got into the neighbor's canola and did tons of damage that Aunt Margaret has to pay for. She's not too happy about it."

"How'd they get out?"

"Two gates were left open. Not one, but two. She says it's Megan's job to move the stock from one pasture to another."

"So it's Megan's fault?"

"Who else?"

Katie opened her notebook.

Cows in Canola—What's that about?

Two gates left open—can't be an accident.

Or can it?

"Hey! Look at that!" Rusty jumped up so fast his sketchbook slid from his lap. It landed on the wicker table, hit Katie's water glass and sent it crashing to the floor. The glass rolled toward her bare toes, spilling water.

She snapped it up and followed Rusty's gaze but caught only a quick glimpse of a shadow that flitted across the shed and was gone. "What did you see?"

"The shadow of a man," Rusty said. "First it was getting bigger, coming this way, and then your glass crashed and the shadow took off."

Katie jumped up, tucked her notebook under her arm and headed for the door. "Let's go!"

The screen door slammed behind them as Katie ran along the driveway with Rusty at her heels. She darted around the corner of the house and followed a gravel path to the backyard. They both stopped abruptly on a small grassy area, cool and green under Katie's bare feet.

They faced a square vegetable garden, divided by narrow grassy paths. It was separated from a field of tall grain by a barbed wire fence. Nothing moved, not so much as a breeze ruffled the tall grasses. The only sound was the high-pitched buzz of crickets.

"Where'd he go?" Rusty whispered.

"I don't know. Maybe it was only your imagination."

"No. Someone was here," Rusty insisted. He started along a narrow pathway between rows of vegetables. At the barbed wire fence he turned left to follow the fence line. Katie ran after him.

As she brushed through long brown grass that grew along the fence line, Katie had the eerie feeling that someone was watching. She glanced up at the house. A thin white face peered down from a second floor window. Megan. Two angry eyes locked with Katie's, and then Megan turned away.

Rusty and Katie followed the barbed wire fence, searching for any sign someone had been here. Then Katie spotted it. Close beside the fence the grasses were trampled, as if by heavy feet. They followed the ragged line of trampled grasses past the vegetable garden to the far side of the house where it stopped abruptly.

A stretch of brown lawn led from that point to the front of the house. They crunched across it, prickly underfoot, and stopped on the driveway. Katie turned toward the road, expecting to see a furtive figure running away.

"Where'd he go?" Rusty asked.

"I don't know. He must be fast."

"Shh!" Rusty whispered. "I think I heard a car door."

They listened. First there was nothing, then an engine came to life somewhere on the road, seeming to come from behind a grove of leafy green trees. Moments later an old, beat-up, red pickup rumbled past the end of the driveway, gathering speed and trailed by a cloud of dust.

7

The house was quiet when Katie first opened her eyes the next morning. Quiet and so breathlessly hot her light cotton pajamas stuck to her skin. She couldn't move her legs. They were trapped, wrapped in a twisted cocoon of sheets. She kicked to free herself. On the far side of the room, Megan moaned softly in her sleep.

For half the night Katie had lain awake, tossing and turning, too hot to fall asleep. Now her eyes were heavy with fatigue, but she couldn't relax. She wanted to be far away from this room when Megan stumbled out of bed with a scowl on her face and a biting comment on her lips.

Katie slid one foot and then the other to the floor. She eased herself up, gathered some clothes and tiptoed from the room. As she made her way down the hallway to the bathroom, she tried not to think about the day ahead. It was too depressing. Stifling heat and whining mosquitoes would drive her half crazy, and boredom would complete the job.

Eyes closed against a stream of warm water that plastered her hair to her head, Katie began to relax. Until suddenly, with a sickening thud, she remembered her birthday. Today. Twelve years old. She turned off the taps and wrapped herself in a towel. She did not want to celebrate her birthday here. What could be worse than sharing a birthday with Megan? Would her cousin have a party? Dozens of Megan clones hanging around the house with weird eyes in skeleton faces? Katie shuddered and tried to think of something else.

She dressed quickly, hung up the towel and left the bathroom.

A sweet, spicy-warm aroma wafted up the stairs. It wrapped itself around her like a silky scarf and gently drew her downward. In the kitchen she stopped, surprised that no one was sitting at the big round table or standing by the old-fashioned sink. The oven light was on, and a mouth-watering scent of cinnamon filled the room, mixed with the rich aroma of freshly brewed coffee.

A murmur of voices and the clink of coffee cups drifted in from the screened porch. Katie tiptoed toward the sounds.

"Allow at least an hour and a half," Aunt Margaret said.

Katie stopped to listen, to figure out what they were talking about. She brushed aside a dark curl from her forehead and wondered why they stopped talking. Then Aunt Margaret was in the doorway with a coffee mug in each hand.

"Well, if it isn't the birthday girl!" She smiled. "Come on out here."

Gram jumped up, threw her arms around Katie and planted a coffee-wet kiss on her cheek. "Happy birthday, Katie! We made cinnamon buns, your favorite. They'll be ready in a few minutes."

"I'm just going to check them." Aunt Margaret bustled past while GJ made his way over to envelop Katie in a birthday hug.

"I hope you won't miss your mom and dad too much," he said.

When the buns were ready, Katie sat at the table and wolfed down two of them, warm and soft and buttery-sweet, while listening to the adults outline their plans for the day.

"Aunt Margaret's taking us into Humboldt," Gram told her. "We can swim and have lunch out. Won't that be fun?"

"Gram told me you don't like the shallow, mucky prairie lakes, Katie," Aunt Margaret said. "But you'll love the indoor pool, no bugs, no slimy bottom. I used to take Megan there a lot when she was younger."

Things were looking up, Katie realized. At least she wouldn't have to spend her entire birthday here, on the farm, with nothing to do. "That sounds like fun." She smiled, but the smile didn't feel quite real.

Aunt Margaret glanced up in the direction of Megan's room. "There's a shopping mall in Humboldt, so I hope Megan will come with us. I want to buy her something new for her birthday."

Real or not, Katie's smile faded. "I hope they've stocked up on black stuff," she said without thinking.

Aunt Margaret laughed. "On the other hand," she said, "if they don't have any black clothes, it'll save me a bundle of money!"

Katie turned to GJ. Her grandfather loved swimming, and he had taught both her and Rusty to swim when they were small. Lately he had been teaching them some fancy dives. "I hope they have a high board," she said. "I could use a diving lesson."

GJ looked surprised, and then a little guilty. "Uh, I'm not coming with you, Katie." He hesitated. "I need to drive into Saskatoon today. There's someone I need to meet."

"Who do you know in Saskatoon?" Katie demanded. What she really meant was, *Who could be more important than going swimming with your granddaughter on her twelfth birthday?*

GJ's eyes shifted to Gram and back to Katie. "Just, uh, a couple of people I've known for a long time. Sorry, Katie, but this is the only day I can go, and it's important to me." He glanced at his watch and stood up. "I need to get going right about now."

Katie ate a third cinnamon bun on the screened porch while GJ's truck rumbled down the driveway. She watched brown dust settle behind the truck and wished she was at home in Victoria.

The day didn't turn out to be a total loss, even though Megan, with an indifferent shrug, agreed to come along. By the time Katie and Rusty were ready to go, Megan was seated in the backseat of Aunt Margaret's ancient little car.

"You get the middle seat," Katie whispered to Rusty.

"No way!"

"Yes way. It's your turn to bond with our dear sweet cousin. Besides, it's my birthday, so I get to choose."

Rusty groaned and slid into the car.

The long drive wasn't completely horrible. Megan actually said a word or two without being forced into it and her usual scowl relaxed into a mild pout. In fact, the closer they got to Humboldt the more Megan began to behave like a real human being. So much so that Katie decided to risk asking a question.

All along the roadsides she noticed swampy, ditch-like wetlands filled with tall brown grasses. Red-winged black birds flitted back and forth. Perched on posts above the shallow water of almost every slough, was one or two of those cylindrical structures, the size of rural mailboxes. Katie wondered what they were. So, when one came up on Megan's side, Katie gathered her courage. "See that mailbox-sized straw thing stuck on a post? What is it anyway?"

Megan looked out the window but didn't answer. Between the two girls, Rusty pulled a face at Katie. His meaning was clear. Why didn't she keep her big mouth shut? Why did she have to stir up trouble?

Slowly Megan's head began to turn. Katie cringed. Rusty leaned toward her, away from Megan. But their cousin smiled. Actually smiled. "They're nest baskets," she said. "We make them for mallards and pintails and teal, but half the time those moronic Canada geese take over."

"Ha!" Rusty said. "I'd like to see a Canada goose squeeze into one of those things! It would have to be as scrawny as..." He leaned further away. "Uh, it would..."

Megan rolled her eyes. "They sit on top."

"You make them?" Katie asked, trying not to look as surprised as she felt.

Megan shrugged. "Used to."

"By yourself?"

Megan's scowl returned. She sank back on the seat and turned away.

"Megan belongs to the Wildlife Federation," Aunt Margaret explained. "She and Scott built several nest baskets and placed them in sloughs near our fields. But since Scott left..." Her voice trailed off.

Megan slouched back against the seat and stared out the window.

Silence gathered inside the little car, relieved only by the high-pitched whine of the engine and the rumble of tires on a gravel road.

Katie chewed her lip. She stared out at the fields they were passing and the faraway horizon. She wanted to ask what Scott stole and how they knew it was him, but decided to wait for a better time. Megan had smiled once today. Who knew? It could happen again.

The good news was that Megan didn't come swimming with them. Gram, Rusty and Katie headed for the pool while Aunt Margaret and Megan hit the mall. Katie hated shopping. Always had. Always would. Sheila hated shopping too; that's one reason they got along so well—used to get along so well, Katie corrected herself—back when they were best friends.

After swimming they met Aunt Margaret and Megan, both of them smiling. Katie stared. She scarcely recognized her cousin and not only because of the smile. Megan had on a new outfit: sandals, pants that came to just below her knees and a shirt that showed her belly button. All of it black, but with a burgundy trim to match her lips. One step toward color.

"Where shall we go for lunch?" Gram asked. "I want to treat my two granddaughters on their birthdays."

Katie really felt like a hamburger and milkshake, but she glanced at Megan and decided not to provoke her. For once her cousin was in a good mood. "You decide," she said. "I've never been to Humboldt before." Once the words were out of her mouth, Katie wondered if she had made a huge mistake. What if Megan didn't want to eat? What if she chose a salad bar? Or worse, a drinking fountain?

"Pizza," Megan said. "I'm starved!"

Would wonders never cease?

8

On the way home Megan curled forward on the seat as if she felt sick. She pressed both hands hard against her flat stomach. "I'm so full!" she moaned. "Why did I go and stuff my face with pizza? I'm as fat as a pig!"

Katie stared at her. "You ate a half slice!"

"And you're scrawny like a stick figure," Rusty added.

"A lot you kids know," Megan growled.

Katie turned away. She stared out the window and wondered what her parents were doing right now. Did they even remember today was her birthday?

If she were home, she'd be in the middle of a party. Laughing with her friends. Opening gifts. Making a wish. Eating chocolate cake. Her eyes stung and her throat ached. She blinked to keep from crying.

Gram and Aunt Margaret chatted louder and more excitedly as they neared the farm. But when Aunt Margaret stopped the car and switched off the engine, they both went quiet and stared at the screen door.

It was Gram who broke the silence. "What shall we make the birthday girls for dinner?" she asked.

"I don't know," Aunt Margaret said. "How about Brussels sprouts and calf's liver?"

"Hey, yeah, Katie's favorite foods!" Rusty grinned.

Megan mumbled something unintelligible and climbed out of the car. She slammed the door behind her.

"Hurry up!" Rusty half pushed Katie out the door.

"What's the big hurry?" She climbed out slowly, wondering why everyone, except Megan, was acting so cheerful all of a sudden. What was there to be cheerful about? And why had Megan stopped on the top stair? Why didn't she go inside?

Even weirder, Gram and Aunt Margaret lingered at the bottom of the stairs. "You go ahead," Gram said to Katie.

Rusty followed like a shadow as Katie stepped around Megan, from brilliant, eye-squinting sunlight into the duller light of the screened porch. Gradually she became aware of three people sitting on the wicker chairs, all of them looking at her and smiling. At the same time she heard an angry murmur of voices in the kitchen. She stopped, confused. Who were all these people?

All three rose to their feet at once. GJ was the tall one, farthest away. The other two were women who seemed to resemble Aunt Margaret, but their faces were difficult to see while Katie's eyes adjusted to the light.

"Surprise!" they yelled.

Katie blinked. One of them moved toward her, arms outstretched. "Happy Birthday, Katie," she cried.

"Mom! How'd you get here? Where's Dad? Is Michael here too?"

Katie's mom hugged her tightly; then she stepped back, smiling. "Okay, one question at a time. Your Aunt Sarah and I flew to Saskatoon this morning, and GJ picked us up. We wanted to surprise you. Of course your dad wanted to come too, but he can't take any time off work right now. He'll phone you tonight for sure. Michael too, they both miss you."

"So why didn't they come too?"

"Well, Katie, plane tickets are so expensive we decided I would come with Aunt Sarah. It's about time we had a family get-together with our big sister and our parents." She glanced toward the door where Gram and Aunt Margaret had squeezed in, pushing Megan in front of them. Then she turned back. "And with you kids too. It seems, for some unknown reason, Aunt Sarah really wanted to see her son. She misses him, if you can believe it!"

"Hey!" Rusty grinned. "I heard that!"

Megan hung back, looking confused and out of place.

"Howdy, all!" Cliff stepped from the kitchen sporting a wide, white-toothed smile. "Happy Birthday, Katie-girl. Another year and you'll be a teenager, like your cousin."

He stepped across the porch, slipped a friendly arm around Megan's shoulders and drew her into the gathering. "And a special Happy Birthday to you, Megan," he said.

Behind Cliff, a girl about Megan's age appeared in the doorway. She had very thick, very straight hair that was cut in short, severe bangs across her forehead. The sides were plastered straight down in front of her ears, making a square frame around her small face. The rest of her hair stuck up like sharp spines on a sea urchin.

The most noticeable thing about her hair, however, was the color. Brilliant purple, a perfect match to her long, cotton sundress. On her feet were purple flip-flops. She had purple toenails and purple finger-nails, but her lips were natural pink.

In contrast to Megan, this girl's face looked fresh and clean. No sign of makeup. Her tanned arms were rounded and muscular, nothing like Megan's bone-thin arms.

Frowning, she pushed her way around Cliff to stand in front of Megan. "Happy Birthday, Megs." She smiled tentatively.

"Thanks, Em." Megan slipped away from Cliff's arm, and the two girls hugged briefly.

"This is Megan's best friend," Aunt Margaret announced. "Emily lives on the farm to the east. She didn't want to miss Megan's birthday, even though they haven't seen too much of each other lately."

"Wait till you see what I got you." Emily's voice sounded strained, as if she wanted to be happy and excited but couldn't quite manage it. She glanced behind Megan at Cliff and then back to her friend.

"I can hardly wait." Megan smiled.

Katie took all of this in and wondered what was going on. Why did Cliff stand there with his arms folded across his chest and glare at Emily as if she were some sort of freak?

Maybe he didn't like the way she looked. Maybe he thought she was a bad influence on Megan.

But Cliff wasn't Megan's father. Was he trying to take the place of Uncle Al?

Dinner turned out to be Katie's absolute all-time favorite. Not calf's liver, but freshly caught salmon her mom had brought in a cooler all the way from Victoria. It was barbequed to perfection by GJ. Along with salmon they had corn on the cob, drizzled with butter, a huge Caesar salad and the most garlicky garlic toast she had ever tasted.

The adults in the family ate and chatted noisily, excited to be together. "When are you going to sell and move out to Victoria, Margaret?" Katie's mom asked. "You live much too far away from the rest of us."

"I may surprise you one of these days," Aunt Margaret said. She looked over at Cliff. "In the meantime, Cliff has been an amazing help since Al died. I honestly don't think we could have managed without him."

Katie stopped listening. She was enjoying her meal too much to be bothered with adult conversation. Butter slid down her chin when she bit into the sweet corn, and she wiped it away with a paper napkin.

Across the table, Megan held her fork in one hand and stared at her plate as if she might throw up any second. To Megan's right, Cliff ate heartily and listened to the adults. On Megan's other side, Emily also ate quickly. She swallowed a bite of corn, wiped her chin and leaned sideways to whisper something to her friend.

Megan nodded, ate one small bite of salmon and glanced at the clock.

During a lull in the conversation Katie's mom turned to Cliff. "Cliff, I really want to thank you on behalf of the entire family. We worry about Margaret struggling to make a go of it out here, so it's good to know she has an assistant she can rely on. You can't imagine how much better that makes us feel."

Cliff smiled modestly. "Well, thank you for saying so, Ma'am. But really, I consider myself lucky to be working here. I studied agriculture at college and farming is something I've always wanted to do."

"Do your parents own a farm too?"

"No, but I wish they did so I could take over one day. They sell farm equipment." He grinned. "And they're most disappointed I took an interest in farming."

While Cliff spoke, Megan calmly put down her fork and pushed her chair back from the table. Without a word she stood and walked out the door to the screened porch. Seconds later the screen door shut with a quiet click. Cliff leaned forward in his chair as if to follow.

"Cliff wants to have his own farm," Emily said. "And he wants it to be this one, don't you, Cliff?"

Cliff shot her an angry glance. He nodded toward Katie's mom. "I have to admit, it's my dream. I want to run a huge operation with all the latest equipment. I've studied the most up-to-date technology and know I can make a go of it. Farming on the prairies today is a big-scale operation. The day of the family farm is long gone. You need to be big to compete. With the right equipment and the best seed available, I could run a couple of sections like this farm without wasting a penny on hired help."

He pushed back his chair. "If you folks will kindly excuse me for a few minutes, I've got to run back to my suite. I'm expecting an important e-mail from a cattle buyer, and I want to see if it's here yet."

He headed for the door at a near run. When he was gone Aunt Margaret laughed nervously. "We seem to be losing people at a great rate," she said. "Do you think it's your cooking, Dad?"

GJ laughed. "Don't think so. I didn't even burn the fish this time. You should see how fast people take off when I serve blackened salmon."

"And he means black." Rusty made a face. "You should try his barbecued chicken. Oh, wait, on second thought, no, you shouldn't!"

"Hey, Rusty, us guys are supposed to stick together through thick and thin!"

"Through thick and thin maybe," Rusty said, "but not through burnt chicken."

Everyone laughed. The phone rang shrill and loud, cutting through the laughter. Katie's eyes flicked to Aunt Margaret, who stiffened at the sound. Her lips still formed a laugh but fear had entered her eyes.

"What is it, Margaret?" Gram asked.

Margaret tried to smile. "Probably just a telemarketer."

Katie pushed herself up from the table and started toward the office. "I'll get it," she said. "I bet it's my dad." She hurried, eager to hear her father's voice.

"No!" Aunt Margaret leapt from her chair and caught up to Katie at the office door. She pushed past Katie and grabbed the phone on the third ring. She clutched it against her ear with both hands.

"Yes?" she whispered.

9

Katie slipped into Aunt Margaret's office and stood quietly listening, aware that behind her the kitchen had gone deathly silent.

"What?" Aunt Margaret's voice exploded into the room. Then, more quietly, "I don't understand." She leaned over her desk and picked up a pen. Moving some loose papers around, she selected one and pulled it closer. She glanced up, spotted Katie, and turned away as if, by looking away, she could prevent Katie from overhearing.

"GM Canola? Of course not. I've never grown it." She scribbled something on the sheet of paper. "Who is this?"

Katie moved closer to the desk. She heard the deep rumble of a man's voice.

Aunt Margaret stopped writing. "How would you possibly know?"

The voice replied, and Aunt Margaret cut in. "Look, I don't know where you got your information, but you're dead wrong. I've never planted it and never intend to, so why would you say such a thing?"

The voice rumbled on, and she laughed bitterly. "If you're trying to blackmail me you're wasting your time because I don't have any money."

Aunt Margaret slammed the phone down. She remained very still, head bowed, her hand still on the receiver. Then she tossed down the pen, crumpled the paper, and threw it in the wastepaper basket. She took a couple of deep breaths to compose herself and started for the door.

"Something's wrong," Katie said. "You know it and I know it. Maybe I can help."

"Oh, Katie. Thank you, but there's nothing you can do."

"You think I'm just a little kid," Katie said. "What you don't realize is that I really am a very successful detective. I've already solved three mysteries this summer."

Aunt Margaret patted Katie's shoulder. "I'm sure you have. But this is not something you should get involved in." She left the room.

Katie dashed to the wastepaper bucket, grabbed the crumpled paper and smoothed it quickly on the desk. She folded it and slid it into the front pocket of her shorts. Then she followed her aunt to the kitchen.

"What's wrong, Margaret?" GJ asked. "You look horrible."

"Gee, thanks, Dad." Aunt Margaret attempted a smile and sank into her chair.

"What your father means," Gram said, "is that you look frightened. What's happened?"

"It's...nothing you can help with."

"Try us," GJ said.

Whatever Aunt Margaret might have said next was cut off by a man's angry shout outside the screen door. "Get off this property before I run you off!"

Katie ran for the door.

"I only wanted to see Megan on her birthday. Is that a crime?" Another male voice answered from farther away.

Katie stopped at the screen door. Partway along the driveway, Cliff waved his fist in the air. "Get out!" he yelled.

A much younger man, a teenager really, faced Cliff from closer to the road. He was tall and thin with long jean-clad legs. His white T-shirt made his tanned arms look rich brown. His sun-bleached hair was inches long on top but cut short and dark over his ears.

Megan stood between the two. "Leave him alone," she growled. "We were only talking."

"If he's not out of here in ten seconds, I'm calling the cops," Cliff yelled.

"Calm down, Cliff, or you'll have a major heart attack." Megan turned back to the teenager. "Please go, Scott. I'll talk to you soon."

"But Megan," he pleaded, "it's your birthday. I thought you and me and Em—"

"Forget it," Cliff broke in. "And get off this property. You're not welcome here."

"Megan?" Scott looked only at her.

"Please just go. I'm going inside to see Emily." Megan stalked along the dusty driveway, pushed past Katie without a glance and shouldered through the crowd gathered at the door.

Shoulders stiff, Scott walked swiftly away. At the road, he turned right and soon disappeared behind the green leafy trees. A door slammed and a noisy engine sputtered into life. A red pickup truck clattered into view and roared angrily down the road in a swirl of dust. The same truck Katie and Rusty had seen the night before.

Cliff turned away. "Hey, Birthday Gal." He smiled, walking toward Katie. "I hope I didn't miss out on cake."

She shook her head. "Why don't you like Scott?"

"I don't trust that kid. If he stole once, he'll do it again, so I don't want him hanging around the place."

"But, are you sure it was him? What did he take?"

Cliff stopped at the door. "Nothing for you to worry about, Katie-girl," he said and stomped into the kitchen.

Katie pulled a face. Why did everyone treat her like a little kid?

"Katie!" Her mom appeared at the door. "Your dad's on the phone."

Katie ran inside. Until today, she hadn't realized how much she missed her dad. She hadn't seen him in almost a month and could hardly wait to hear his voice. As she ran through the kitchen, it occurred to her that until last week when they visited his Alberta ranch, Sheila hadn't seen her own father in close to a year.

Then she heard her dad's familiar voice. "Happy Birthday, Katie! I wish I was there with you."

The second Katie emerged from Aunt Margaret's office the kitchen exploded in inharmonious song. On the table, two cakes blazed with twinkling candles. Mouths opened and closed, teeth and the whites of eyes flickered in candlelight while Katie waited awkwardly for the birthday song to end. On the far side of the room, Megan leaned sullenly against the kitchen doorway. Aunt Margaret watched as if afraid her daughter might make a run for the door.

At last the song screeched to an end with, "Happy Birthdays Dear Megan-and-Katie, Happy Birthdays to you."

Katie swooped over to see her cake and examine the presents piled on the table.

She blew out every candle and ate a huge piece of her chocolate cake with thick, dark chocolaty icing. Then she tried a slice of Megan's carrot cake. It tasted spicy and sweet and surprisingly good. Not at all like a carrot. Across the table, Megan nibbled on some crumbs but avoided the icing. The sliver of cake looked almost intact when she pushed her plate away.

"How about some of this chocolate cake?" GJ slid a slice toward Megan. "It's absolutely delicious."

Megan looked at it and licked her lips. For a moment, Katie thought she might actually take a bite. But she pushed it away too. "No thanks," she said. "I'm way too full."

"We should come here every year," Rusty said. "Where else can you get two birthday cakes at once?" He ate quite happily, ignoring the foul looks from both of his cousins.

Katie didn't wait for the others to finish their cake. She started opening her presents. A fancy new notebook with a hardcover and a pocket for tucking in important papers (or evidence) came from her grandparents. Inside the front cover were slots that held a pocket-sized notepad, pen, pencil, eraser, magnifying glass and calculator.

Aunt Margaret gave her a Swiss Army knife. "Because," she said, "you never know when it might come in handy."

Rusty's parents, Aunt Sarah and Uncle Jason, gave her a book called, *Crimes of the Century*. She could hardly wait to read it. And from Rusty came a small, compact flashlight. She switched it on and shone it in his face.

Rusty put his hand up to shade his eyes. "I thought you could use a new one," he said. "Since your old one got kind of bashed up when you dropped it down that tunnel on my head."

"It landed on the rocks beside you, not on your head. But, thanks, Rusty." She switched it off and slipped it into her pocket alongside the paper from Aunt Margaret's office. "It's nice and small but it's bright too." She almost added that it would be perfect for investigating crime scenes but caught herself in time. She had promised to stay out of trouble this summer. Unfortunately, to her parents' and grand-parents' way of thinking, investigating crimes was not the ideal way to go about it.

Her parents gave her a cell phone. "Wow! That's exactly what I wanted!"

"We figured you could use it in case you find your-self in trouble again. At least you can phone for help," said her mom.

"Thanks, Mom." Katie pushed the power button and waited for the little screen to light up. She fid-dled with the phone for a few minutes, pushing but-tons to see how it worked. "It takes pictures too!" she grinned. "That will come in handy!"

There was one more present on the table. Katie picked it up and read the card.

Happy Birthday, Katie. I'll be thinking of you today.

Miss you,

Sheila.

Katie tore open the paper and found a new mys-tery novel by her favorite author. She held it in her hands and thought about Sheila, her ex-best friend. But maybe Sheila wasn't a deserter at all, maybe she just really needed some time with her dad.

"You can phone Sheila on your new cell phone and thank her," Mom suggested.

"Yeah," Katie said, "I will." She glanced at the clock. "But she'll be out on the range riding Silver right now. She likes to go with her dad after dinner." Katie smiled, knowing she would talk to Sheila soon; maybe they could still be best friends after all.

"Let's try the phone to be sure it works," Mom suggested. "Why don't you phone Megan on her cell?"

Katie shook her head. "I don't know the number."

Cliff got to his feet and nodded to Katie's and Rusty's mothers. "It was wonderful meeting you two lovely ladies, and I hope you enjoy your visit to Saskatchewan. I thank you all for a wonderful meal, but I really must go now, I've got chores waiting."

While their moms smiled happily after Cliff, Katie looked at Rusty and rolled her eyes. Rusty opened his mouth and jabbed a finger toward his throat. They both grinned.

"I don't have my phone," Megan jumped up, patting her empty waistband. "I left it to recharge in Mom's office last night and forgot it when we went to Humboldt." She disappeared into the office and came running out a second later. "It's not there!"

"It's Scott again." Cliff lingered at the door. "He must have taken it when no one was home today."

"Why would he do that?" Katie asked. "It doesn't make any sense."

"Why does he do half the things he does? Maybe he wants to check Megan's calls to see who's been phoning her. I'm sure it's him. Seems to me I saw a phone just like Megan's clipped to his belt when he was outside."

"You're wrong," Megan told him. "Scott didn't have a cell phone on him. I was there too, remember?"

Cliff took a step toward her. "Your mother told you to stay away from that boy. Can't you understand he's stalking you? He could be dangerous."

Megan backed toward the stairs. "Who do you think you are?" she screeched. "My father?" She turned and ran up the stairs.

"Megan, come back here!" Cliff yelled and started after her.

"It's all right, Cliff, let her go," Aunt Margaret said. "No sense in letting her spoil everyone's fun."

That was the most sensible thing Katie had heard all day. She smiled when Megan's bedroom door slammed and the sound of it reverberated through the house.

"And I really don't think Scott is dangerous," Aunt Margaret continued. "He's just a boy who made a mistake. As for Megan's cell phone, she's forever misplacing it. I'm sure it will show up soon."

Once again, Cliff headed for the door.

"Why don't we get Katie to try the number now?" GJ suggested. "If it rings we can track it down. What's the number?"

Aunt Margaret gave Katie the number, and she started to punch it in. Not that she wanted her first call on her new cell phone to be to her cousin, but she was curious to find out where the phone had gone. You never knew what might turn out to be a clue.

"If it rings, say hello to Scott," Cliff called over his shoulder.

Katie pushed Send. They didn't hear the phone ringing anywhere in the house. After four rings, Megan's voice answered, "Hey, it's Megan. Leave a message. If you're real lucky, I'll get back to you."

10

"I should go." Emily's mouth twisted down on one side. "I don't think, like, Megan wants me here?"

"I'm really sorry, Emily," Aunt Margaret said. "I don't know what's gotten into Megan lately; she's acting just plain rude. But I poured you some tea. Why don't you stay and finish it? We enjoy your company even if Megan is too preoccupied with herself right now."

"I can help you clean up," Emily suggested with an unhappy glance at stacks of dishes piled on the countertop and overflowing the sink.

"Thanks, but no." Aunt Margaret grinned. "That's what my sisters are here for."

Katie's mom and Aunt Sarah groaned.

"Katie," said her mom, "why don't you and Rusty take Emily out to the porch? There's no need for her to rush off just yet, and you kids can keep her company while we get these dishes done."

"Good idea." Katie hopped up from the table. She couldn't believe her luck. There were tons of unanswered questions rattling around in her brain and this opportunity to question Megan's friend was perfect timing. She grabbed her new notebook and cell phone and headed for the door before anyone could have a change of mind.

Emily carried her tea out and sat on a chair next to Katie. Resting her elbows on the white wicker arms, Emily stared into the mug she clutched in both hands. Rusty sauntered out and plunked himself down on the chair closest to the door, his sketchbook balanced on his knees.

"So, Emily," Katie began, "have you and Megan been friends for a long time?"

Emily nodded. "Ever since we were three years old. Our parents were, like, I mean, friends too."

"They aren't anymore?"

Emily shook her purple, sea urchin hair. "I don't know. Since Megan's dad died, they don't see each other so much. Megan's mom is always, like, way too busy." She sipped her tea and muttered something under her breath.

"Are you mad because Megan hardly paid any attention to you tonight?"

"Why be mad?" she sighed. "I'm getting used to it. Megan doesn't like, uh, like me so much anymore."

"So, you don't hang out together?" Katie clutched her notebook on her lap, itching to take notes but afraid to open it. Sooner or later Emily would get tired of answering questions, just like everyone did. And if Emily saw Katie writing down everything she said, it would be sooner rather than later.

"Not like we used to. Summers used to be, like, so much fun. Megs, Scott and me always got together with kids from school and went swimming or biking, whatever. And we played tons of baseball." Emily smiled, remembering. "Megs was good too. You should have seen her hit that ball!"

Her smile vanished. "But Megan never wants to do anything anymore. And she's been tons worse since Cliff fired Scott."

"I thought Aunt Margaret fired him."

"Huh? No, it was Cliff."

"But, why?"

"Scott was staying here to help with seeding, and he slept in the spare room in Cliff's suite. They were real busy, so Megan was supposed to, like, take care of the housekeeping in their rooms? But she got too busy with exams. Anyway, her mom went in to clean one day and found something in Scott's room."

"What was it?"

"A necklace. She didn't even know it was, like, missing? It used to belong to Megan's grandma–her dad's mother? Anyway, before she died Grandma Piercy gave the necklace to Megan's mom."

"So, is it, like, valuable or what?" Katie was vaguely aware that *like* had slipped into her sentence. Seemed like *like* was catchy.

"I guess so. It's old anyway. I think it's, like, a family heirloom or something? From England. Anyway, Megan's mom kept it in her jewelry box in her bedroom, but she never wore it. She doesn't like, uh, jewelry."

"But, why would Scott take it?"

"I wouldn't have believed it a few months back, but who knows? It's totally weird how everyone around here has changed lately. Megan sure did. And Scott's so desperate to save money for college, maybe he planned on selling the necklace to make a bundle."

"Then, why would he leave it in his room? You'd think he'd be smart enough to figure out Aunt Margaret would find it."

Emily shrugged. "Haven't a clue. Maybe he felt guilty about taking it in the first place. I mean, he really likes Megan, and her mom's always been real good to him. She even gave him a job to help him make some money." She sipped her tea and thought for a minute. "So, yeah, maybe that's it. Maybe he couldn't go through with it but, like, got caught before he could return the necklace."

"But Megan still sees Scott?"

"Yeah, sometimes, when she can get away from here."

"Why can't she get away?"

Emily frowned and stared out through the window screen. Katie was sure she'd had enough and wouldn't answer any more questions, but Emily surprised her. Maybe she was happy to share her worries. Still gazing outside, Emily said, "Megan's mom won't let her see Scott and she keeps a close eye on everything Megs does, 'cause she thinks Megan might, like, sneak off."

Emily gulped her tea and lowered the mug to her knee, still holding it in both hands. "Then there's Cliff. That guy watches over Megs too, like he's her big brother or something? It drives her nuts! Tonight, when I caught him alone in the kitchen, I told him to back off. He got real mad. He thinks I'm, like, a freak."

"So that's what you were arguing about when we got back?"

Emily nodded.

Katie couldn't stand it any longer. She opened her notebook and started to write.

Emily twisted her head to see. "What are you, some kind of spy?"

"No." Katie shook her head without looking up. "A detective. And a good one too. Ask Rusty."

Emily turned to Rusty.

Rusty looked up from his drawing and pulled a face. "I have to admit, she's not bad." He grinned. "And you gotta admire her modesty."

Emily's eyes shifted back to Katie. "I don't know what you're detecting but if you can help Megan, count on me to help. Can you believe I had to whisper a message to her tonight? Scott wanted to meet her but he was scared to call her cell phone because her mom keeps track of the calls when she gets the bill."

Katie smiled as she made a note. She felt good. Emily was the first person over twelve ever to take her seriously. "What makes you think Megan needs help?"

"I don't know. I just figure something's, like, really wrong and Megs can't handle it herself." Emily's mouth twisted. "But she won't talk to me about it, that's for sure. Or Scott either. We're kinda worried she might have, like, anorexia nervosa."

"Anorexia nervosa?" Rusty snorted. "What's that? Some kind of dinosaur?"

"No, Dumbo," Katie said, "it means she will eat hardly anything because she thinks she's fat. We talked about it at school last year."

"Megan? Fat? She looks like a walking skeleton."

"Anorexia is an eating disorder," Emily explained. "I looked it up on the web. It's, like, something wrong with the dopamine receptors in the brain. Or, whatever. Seems like it's mostly girls who get it and they, like, basically stop eating. It's like the only way they can control their lives is to not eat. If they eat anything, they feel guilty, even if it's just like, salad or something. And they never stop exercising."

"How come they don't starve to death?" Katie wondered, thinking about Megan's bone-thin arms.

"That's the thing. No matter how skinny they get, they still aren't happy. They're hungry but can't admit it. Some girls get to the point where they can't eat, even to save their own lives."

"That's sick!" Rusty said.

"Yeah," Emily agreed. "It's, an illness, you know? One thing I read said anorexia has, like, the highest death rate of any psychiatric disease."

"Whoa!" Rusty said. "That explains why she's skinny like a bone and grumpy as a turtle."

"A turtle?" Katie asked.

"Yeah, you know those snapping turtles? When they're hungry, they snap at anything that comes near them. And Megan is hungry all the time."

Katie rolled her eyes and turned back to Emily.

"Just ignore him," she said. "He's way weird."

"But he's right." Emily's eyes misted over. "That's exactly Megan. She's always hungry, but she won't eat. She's wasting away."

Emily drained her mug, placed it on the wicker table and stood up. "I don't know how to help her. And her mom's so busy worrying about the farm, she doesn't even notice anything's wrong." She started for the door. "I need to, like, thank Megan's mom for inviting me. Then I'm gone."

"Wait!" Katie said. "Could you help me meet up with Scott? I need to question him."

Emily turned back, a half smile on her lips. "You sure do like asking questions, don't you?" She rested her hand on the doorjamb. "Okay, give me your cell number and I'll, like, call you tomorrow."

Katie opened her phone to check the number then wrote it on the small pad tucked in the front pocket of her new notebook. She ripped off the sheet and handed it to Emily.

After Emily rattled off in her parents' battered blue truck, Katie and Rusty remained on the porch. Katie wrote notes on everything Emily had told her, a crucial part of any investigation, so she wouldn't forget the smallest detail.

In some remote part of her mind Katie realized Rusty was bent over his sketchbook. She began to wonder what he was drawing. She looked up. He was lost in his work, sketching furiously.

Rusty had always loved to draw, and even though Katie would hate to admit it to him, she admired his skill. She knew he never wanted anyone to see a drawing until it was done and she respected that. So she tried to resist standing up and moving close enough for a good look.

Her good intentions lasted for at least ten seconds. Then she reminded herself that, like all good detectives, she was born to snoop. She stood, stepped closer to Rusty and managed a quick glimpse of a tall slim figure with hair that stood long on top of his head but was cut bluntly over his ears.

"You're drawing Scott?"

Rusty covered his work, but his smile told Katie he was pleased she had recognized the figure. "I'm training myself to draw faces from memory."

"Why?"

He shrugged. "I dunno. Something to do. It makes me more observant."

"Just faces?"

Rusty shook his head. "No, the whole person, clothes, everything."

"Can I see? Please?"

He narrowed his eyes. "Why?"

"Because," she hesitated. "Okay, your drawings are good, Rusty. I like seeing them. Besides, I want to compare it with my notes about Scott."

"Why?"

"I'll tell you after I see it."

Rusty leaned over his work, pencil in hand. "Maybe, in a minute, when I'm done."

Katie sat back down and tried to concentrate on her notes. A clatter of dishes and the chatter of voices that drifted from the kitchen told her the rest of the family would soon wander out here. There wasn't much time. She tapped her foot impatiently until at last Rusty put his pencil down. Katie snapped her notebook shut. "Can I see it now?"

Rusty shrugged. "I guess." He held his sketchbook toward her.

Katie studied the drawing. A tall young man looked up at her, remarkably like Scott, right down to his white T-shirt and jeans that were a bit too short for his long legs.

"What about the cell phone?" she asked.

Rusty frowned, thinking. "I don't remember a phone," he admitted.

"Me neither. Cliff must be more observant than us."

She sighed, "You know what? I'm so full I feel sick. Want to walk up the driveway with me?"

"Why?"

"I told you, I'm full from eating too much cake, so I need some exercise."

"Ha! I bet you want to see where that red truck was parked."

There was no point in denying it; Rusty knew her too well. "Okay, I might want to do that too, but I really am full, aren't you?"

Rusty put down his book and patted his stomach. "Yeah, kind of. If I'm going to eat more cake later, I need some exercise."

They walked the length of the driveway, swatting mosquitoes with every step. The evening air was hot and sleepy. It smelled like dust. At the road they turned right and walked to a grove of poplars that grew just inside the barbed wire fence bordering Aunt Margaret's farm. Between the fence and the road was a small slough where red-winged blackbirds balanced on the tips of tall brown reeds. The birds filled the air with squeaky little songs and fluttered their short black wings. Here and there red shoulder patches flashed bright in the evening sunlight that filtered through the trees.

Long green grass grew alongside the slough but turned brown near the dirt road where the kids stood. Two wide tracks of flattened grass made a wide semicircle away from the road and back again.

"If Scott parked here," Rusty said, "he was on the wrong side of the road. I'm going to check out the other side." He ran across the road.

Katie bent to study the tire imprints on the grass.

Rusty's footsteps thudded back across the dirt. "Nothing's been parked over there," he said.

"No," Katie said. "His truck would be better hidden on this side."

A short shrill whistle made Katie's breath catch in her throat. It was followed by loud flapping, like a strong gust of wind catching an awning. Every blackbird took to the air in an instant.

"What the heck was that?" Rusty whispered.

The whistle sounded again; then more flapping and a huge splash. The kids turned toward the slough in time to see a large, brown speckled duck land in the water, wings fluttering.

They moved down the slope. "Look at that!" Katie pointed. "Another nest basket, like the one by the hay field." Directly above the duck, the man-made nest was partially hidden by reeds, but she could see that it was made of long grasses tightly wound around a wide cylinder made of chicken wire.

A second duck swam over. It had a brown head, pure white chest and neck, and a dark back and tail, but its most noticeable feature was its long pointed tail feathers.

"That must be the male," Rusty said.

Katie nodded. "What's that lying in the grass?" She crouched at the edge of the slough and worked to free a small section of chicken wire entangled in the long green grass.

"It's the same as the stuff in the equipment shed."

"And the wire that got caught in the cutter bar." Katie looked across the shallow water. "I wonder who made that nest basket?" She climbed back up toward the road, searching the grass for other chunks of wire that might have been dropped. She stopped abruptly. "Look at this!" Close beside one of the tire prints, at the edge of the long grass, lay a small closed cell phone.

"Hey! Weird." Rusty picked it up. It had a black leather case with a large plastic clip on the back. Rusty opened it and the little screen lit up.

"It still works, so it hasn't been here for long," Katie said. "Hold on, I have an idea."

She opened her own phone and pushed a few buttons until the word *Redial?* popped up on her screen. She pushed Send.

Seconds later a raucous tune filled the air. It stopped. And started again. Rusty stared at the phone in his hand. "It's ringing! What do I do?"

"Answer it."

The phone rang once more before Rusty figured out which button to push. He put the phone to his ear. "Hello?" he said nervously.

"Hi, Rusty," Katie said. "What's new?"

Rusty pulled a face and disconnected. "So, it's Megan's phone!" he said. "Cliff was right. Scott must have taken it. He must have chucked it out after he was done. But why?"

Katie closed her phone. "I don't know."

"Look who's coming!" Rusty said.

Broad shoulders hunched forward, muscular arms hanging out from his sides like a gunslinger's, Cliff strode down the center of the road toward them. "What are you kids doing there?" he yelled.

11

"Let's get out of here," Rusty whispered. His face turned so pale the sprinkling of freckles across his nose and cheeks stood out in pink blotches.

"Why? We aren't doing anything wrong."

Katie stepped sideways to place herself between the rapidly approaching man and her cousin. "Don't let him see the cell phone," she whispered over her shoulder. "Stick it in your pocket."

"I don't have a pocket!"

"Then clip it to your belt. Face it away; hide it behind your hands."

"What belt?"

"Rusty!"

"Okay, okay. But I don't know why. I still say we should run."

"Too late."

Cliff's heavy workboots sent up little puffs of dust

with every step. His face looked tight and angry. He didn't slow down until the toes of his boots almost touched Katie's sandals. She curled her toes and refused to step back.

Cliff towered over the two kids. "What are you doing here?" he repeated, more quietly this time.

"Walking," Katie said. "We were way full from pigging out on birthday cake and we needed some exercise."

"So we can eat more cake later," Rusty added.

"Then what are you doing with that wire?" he nodded suspiciously at Katie's hand.

Katie glanced down, surprised to see she was still holding the chunk of chicken wire. "Nothing," she said. "I found it down there," she pointed toward the slough, "and we kind of wondered how it got there."

The anger faded from his eyes. "Sorry, kids. When I saw you with that wire in your hands, I thought you were putting it here."

"Why would we do that?"

A sheepish smile played around the corners of his mouth. "You're right: I wasn't thinking. It's just that so many odd things have happened around here lately, I guess I'm on edge." Cliff took several steps toward the slough and then stopped and glanced around, hands on his hips. The curved red handles of a small tool protruded from the back pocket of his jeans. "Where exactly did you find it?" he asked.

"Down there. See? Where the grass is disturbed." Before Cliff could ask any more questions, Katie asked one of her own. "Why are you out here anyhow? I thought you had work to do."

"I have stacks of work," he said impatiently. "But first I needed to check on the stock, so I went to the pasture to be sure the cows were all right. After I saw Scott lurking in the area I wanted to be sure he hadn't left the gates open again."

"Does he do that a lot?"

"I know he did it once before. That kid's a troublemaker. I said so from the beginning, but no one would believe me."

"How did you know it was him?"

"How come you ask so many questions?" Cliff asked, but his broad smile took away any sting from his words. He glanced sympathetically from Katie to Rusty. "I guess it must be kind of boring around here for you two kids. Maybe I can find something to keep you busy."

"No thanks!" Rusty said. "That's what my dad says when he wants me to do chores. Trust me, we aren't that bored."

Cliff threw his head back and laughed. "Fair enough. But now, I really must get to work. Why don't you two run along to the house? There are a couple of things I need to do here before heading back."

Suddenly the air was filled with the quick raucous notes of a song.

"What's that?" Cliff glanced around. "Where's it coming from?"

"I think it's my cell," Katie pulled the phone from her pocket and moved closer to Rusty.

The loud music blared out again.

"It's not yours." Cliff moved toward Rusty. "What's that clipped to your waistband?"

Rusty glanced down. "Oh!" he said. "I forgot I had my cell with me." He tried to pull it free of his black shorts, but it seemed stuck there. The music blared out again.

"Unclip it," Katie said. "Hurry up and answer. I bet it's your mom."

"Don't you know how to use your own phone?" Cliff's eyes narrowed and he moved closer. "Are you sure it's even yours?"

"Here, let me help." Katie stepped between Rusty and Cliff.

"I'm okay," Rusty said. He wrenched the phone

free, flipped it open, ran his finger over the buttons and finally pushed one.

"Mom?" he said.

"Yeah, I'm okay."

"Just talking to Cliff."

"Uh, I don't know."

"Sure. We'll be there in a few minutes."

He closed the cell. "Our moms want us to come back now."

Cliff eyed him suspiciously. "That phone looks exactly like Megan's. And it plays the same tune."

"Yeah? Then, I guess we share the same good taste."

"Must be because they're cousins," Katie said. "Did you notice they both like to wear black?"

As the kids walked away, side by side, Katie felt Cliff's eyes boring into her back, but she didn't dare look until they reached the driveway. Cliff hadn't moved. Arms folded across his chest, he kept a wary eye on them, as if he suspected they were up to no good. She leaned toward Rusty. "Who was on the phone?"

"Don't know. Some guy, probably Scott."

Katie walked a few more steps, expecting Rusty to fill in the details, but he said nothing. "So?" she asked. "What did he say?"

Rusty stopped. "Uh, let me think..."

"Can't you think and walk at the same time? Cliff's watching us."

Rusty started walking, more slowly than before. He gazed up at the huge dome of sky. "Okay, here's how it went down."

Went down, Katie repeated to herself, pleased to hear Rusty using some detective-type talk.

"When I answered the phone, I said, 'Mom?' Because, you said it must be Mom, so I pretended it was."

Katie nodded.

"So, anyway, the voice sounded surprised. He said, 'Megan, you okay? You sound real weird. Sorry for using your cell, but I was worried.'"

"So, I said, 'Yeah, I'm okay.'"

"Then the voice got mad. 'Where's Megan?' he asked."

"'Just talking to Cliff,' I told him."

"The voice stopped being mad and sounded all worried instead. 'Is she okay? When will she be back? Why didn't she take her phone?'"

"He asked those three questions so fast I didn't know what to say, so I just said, 'Uh, I don't know.'"

"That's perfect; it answers all three questions at once. Then what?"

"Uh, I can't remember. What else did I say?"

Being an accomplished eavesdropper, Katie was proud of her excellent memory. "You said, 'Sure. Be there in a few minutes.'"

"Oh yeah. Cliff was starting to look kinda mad. I don't think he believed us about the phone, so I wanted him to think our moms were waiting for us. When the voice said, 'You must be one of Megan's cousins. Tell her I'll talk to her later,' I improvised."

"Hey, Rusty," Katie slapped her cousin on the back, "you did great!"

Rusty grinned.

"I'll make a good assistant out of you yet," she added.

For a second Rusty looked crushed; then his grin returned. "Partner is more like it."

They were almost at the house by then, but there was something Katie needed to do before they went inside. "Okay, partner, what do you suggest we do next?"

"I don't know. Go inside and give Megan's phone back? We need to tell her Scott took it and dumped it by his truck."

"What if it wasn't him?"

"Of course it was him. We saw him drive away from there, didn't we? Besides, he said he used it, I just told you that."

Katie nodded. "He meant that he was sorry for calling Megan's cell because he's not supposed to. But that's the point. If he knew Megan didn't have the phone, why would he call her on it?"

"Uh, to make it look good when someone else found it and checked the incoming calls?"

"Maybe, but that seems kinda dumb. If Scott didn't want to get caught, why not toss it into the slough where no one would ever find it?"

Rusty thought for a minute. "I know! Because he likes Megan and he doesn't want to wreck her cell phone?"

Katie wrinkled her forehead—she'd never thought of that. "I'm still not sure it was Scott, because why would he take it in the first place?"

Rusty bit his lip, thinking, and then his face lit up. "Okay, then. You think Megan's so spaced out she dropped it herself and forgot she even had it with her?"

Katie shrugged. "Could be. Or..."

"Or what?"

"If you were my partner I wouldn't have to tell you, you'd know."

"Uh-uh. Partners share their ideas."

Katie smiled. "All right then. We'll share later. But before we go inside we need to check Megan's cell phone and see what other calls have been made this evening."

Katie glanced over her shoulder. Cliff was starting up the driveway. "Let's go into the trailer."

Katie closed the trailer door, and Rusty opened the cell phone. He found the Menu button and then the number of the call he had answered.

Katie jotted the number in her notebook. "We'll check the phone book and see if it was Scott."

Then they looked through the outgoing calls. The last number seemed familiar somehow, and Katie jotted it down too. "I think it might be Aunt Margaret's number. I'll check when we go in."

"Or we could hit Redial."

Katie frowned. "Exactly what I was thinking."

They leaned their heads close over the phone, listening as it rang once, twice, three times. Then someone picked up. After a long silence, a barely audible voice whispered, "Yes?"

"Is it Aunt Margaret?" Rusty whispered.

Katie nodded. "I think so."

"What do you want from me?" the voice asked, and Katie was sure then that it was Aunt Margaret. "Do you think I can't hear you whispering? Why don't you just leave me alone? It's hard enough trying to get by without you constantly harassing me. If you want something, why don't you come right out and tell me instead of making these constant calls and ridiculous accusations?"

Rusty put his finger over the key to disconnect, but Katie pushed his hand away. "Not yet," she whispered.

"It's not going to work," Aunt Margaret said. "I've had enough. If you're planning to blackmail me, good luck! I haven't got a penny."

She paused. "So now you're just going to breathe into the phone like a pervert?" The phone slammed down hard.

"Ouch!" Rusty pulled the phone away from his ear.

"So," Katie said, "we know where that call to Aunt Margaret came from earlier."

"Right," Rusty agreed. "Megan's cell. And we know who made it. What I don't get is why? I mean, maybe Scott's out to get revenge, but this is a really dumb way to get it if you ask me. What good does it do him?"

"Actually, we need to be sure of the who before we can figure out the why," Katie said. She peeked through the half-closed blinds toward the house, half expecting to see Cliff waiting for them near the screen door. But there was no sign of him. "Let's go inside," she said. "But don't tell anyone about the phone, not until we talk to Megan. Turn it off so it won't ring."

"But, they'll see it when we go in."

"Then grab some clothes or something to take with you."

"I don't need anything."

"I know that, Rusty. But you can wrap the phone up so no one sees it. Besides, if anyone saw us come in here, they'll want to know why. So we'll both take something with us, okay?" Katie pulled open her drawer and grabbed a T-shirt and a pair of shorts.

Rusty grabbed some clothes too.

"Let's go," Katie said. She pushed open the trailer door, stuck her head out and looked both ways before stepping outside. She had a terrible feeling that Cliff was lurking nearby, somewhere just out of sight. It seemed that nothing happened on this farm without Cliff knowing about it, and as long as they had Megan's cell phone, he would be watching them. Did he think they stole it from the office? Or, was he somehow involved?

12

Katie stopped behind the trailer where she had a good view of the driveway. "Wait," she whispered, "stay close."

"Why?" Rusty kept walking.

"Because I think Cliff is waiting for us."

"Well, that doesn't take a whole lot of detective power to figure out."

Katie followed his gaze toward the house. Like an apparition, Cliff stood just inside the screen door. Only the pale skin of his face showed through the gray veil of the screen, and his white arms were folded across his chest.

Cliff pushed open the door, his lips curled in a crooked smile. "Hi kids," he said, his voice friendly and welcoming. "Come on in real quick and leave those darned mosquitoes outside where they belong."

He held the door for them. Rusty squeezed quickly

past, and then it was Katie's turn. She avoided Cliff's eyes and ducked under his arm. He must have been telling the truth earlier, she thought, he really must have been in the cow pasture because he smelled like a warm cow flop. She held her breath and hurried toward a friendly murmur of voices in the kitchen.

The room fell silent as the kids entered. GJ, Gram, Katie's mom and her two aunts each had a tea mug in front of them on the table. Each face looked up with an identical expression, all of them wrinkled with worry. But Aunt Margaret was the only one whose eyes were red and watery.

"What's up?" Katie asked.

"Nothing," her mom said. "We're just talking. Catching up on each other's lives."

"But," Katie persisted, "it looks like something's wrong."

Aunt Margaret stood and walked to the sink. She grabbed a tissue, leaned against the counter and gazed out the window. She blew her nose with a great, loud honk. "I must have a touch of hay fever," she said.

"Where have you kids been?" Aunt Sarah asked. "We were about to call you."

Katie was distracted by a distinct cow smell that floated around her nostrils. The warm sharp scent of manure and sweat and straw came from directly behind her. This could be trouble, she realized. She sidled closer to the table, thinking quickly. "We walked to the road," she said vaguely, "and that's where we talked to Cliff. Then, on the way back, we went into the trailer to get some clothes."

When in doubt, tell the truth. But would it be enough to satisfy Cliff?

Rusty's mom nodded. "Don't wander off too far," she said. "You don't know your way around here, and we wouldn't want you to get lost."

"How could we get lost when we can see every little bump in the ground for a hundred miles?" Rusty asked.

His mom laughed and pushed her chair back. "How about you and I go for a walk together?" she said. "I need some time to visit with my son."

Rusty grinned. "Sure, Mom. Then, when we get back, I'll be ready for more cake."

Katie relaxed. Everything was going to be fine.

Behind her, Cliff cleared his throat. "Even if Rusty did manage to get lost," he said. "He can always use his cell phone to call for help, so there's really no need to worry."

Aunt Sarah glanced up at Cliff in surprise. "Katie has a cell phone," she explained. "She just got it for her birthday. But Rusty doesn't, not yet, although I have to admit it seems like a good idea. These two are forever getting themselves into trouble."

"If he doesn't have a cell," Cliff sounded puzzled, "how did you just talk to him?"

Aunt Sarah frowned. "What do you mean?"

"I mean, a few minutes ago when I ran into the kids by the road. Rusty had a cell clipped to his shorts. After it rang and he talked, he told me it was you."

Aunt Sarah walked over to her son. "What's he talking about, Rusty?"

Clutching his little bundle of clothes against his stomach, Rusty stared at the floor. He shifted from one foot to the other.

Aunt Sarah looked over his shoulder. "Cliff?"

"You know, I thought that phone looked like Megan's. It played the same so-called music too. But Rusty said the phone belonged to him."

"Rusty, let me see what you have there." Aunt Sarah held out her hands.

Rusty glanced down at the crumpled bundle in his hands and then at Katie. He handed over the clothes to his mom.

She carefully unwrapped the cell phone and stared at it in surprise. "Russell," she said, "it's time to start explaining. And I need to hear the truth."

Katie started for the stairs, hoping no one would notice.

"Katie!" her mom called. "We need you here for this."

She stopped. Turned around. Opened her mouth.

"No," her mom said. "You be the silent partner this time."

Rusty licked his lips. "Okay. I admit it, we found the cell phone. It was lying in the grass by the road." He nodded in that direction. "Up near those trees. Anyhow, we figured Scott had parked his truck there and maybe he took the phone, like Cliff said, and then tossed it away."

"Or maybe Megan had it and dropped it by mistake," Katie added.

"Let Rusty finish," Katie's mom said sharply.

"So then, uh...," Rusty paused. "Then I picked it up and I was going to bring it back to Megan. But suddenly Cliff showed up and..." He glanced at Katie. "I'm not sure what happened after that."

Every eye turned to Katie. Her mind whirled. There had to be a logical explanation.

"Katie?" her mom asked.

"Oh. Am I allowed to talk now?"

"Please do."

"Okay then. Well—here's the thing." She took a

deep breath and let her eyes roam slowly from face to face. "Uh—like Rusty said, we found the phone in the grass." When in doubt, tell the truth. "So then I dialed Megan's number, on my phone, to see if it would ring. Turned out it did, so we were going to bring it back. Then Cliff came charging up and yelled at us. He looked real mad, and we got kind of, you know, scared."

"Me?" Cliff chuckled. "Scary?"

Katie plunged on with her story. "So when the phone rang, I sort of told Rusty to pretend it was Aunt Sarah. That way Cliff would think you wanted us to come back right away. And Rusty did good too, he really sounded as if he was talking to you."

"And after that Cliff got real nice," Rusty added.

Now every eye shifted to Cliff.

He shook his head, laughing. "I don't believe this! Okay, sure I was mad at first when I saw the kids with that chicken wire, but I apologized for that. And when I saw Rusty with that phone, I was almost sure he was lying, but I gave him the benefit of the doubt. You know me, I'm one of the least scary guys in the world. If you want scary, look at Scott Holden. He took Megan's cell, and I mean to find out why." Cliff swung around on his heel and stomped out the door.

It was GJ who broke the silence following Cliff's departure. "Well," he said, "no harm done. And that was quick thinking kids. It's good to know you can handle yourselves if you believe there's a problem."

"Even if it was only Cliff," Aunt Margaret added. "He's the nicest young man you could ever hope to meet." She turned to Rusty's mom. "Sarah, why don't you and Rusty go off on that walk now? And Laura, you must be wanting to spend some time with Katie. I'm going to take that cell phone upstairs and have a chat with my own daughter."

Katie watched her aunt start up the stairs and forced her feet not to follow. She wanted to press her ear to Megan's door and listen. She wanted to ask...

"Katie?"

She turned to face her mom. "Katie, didn't you hear me? I asked if you want to go out to the porch where we can sit and chat?"

Katie glanced back up the stairs. "Sure, okay."

Her mom smiled and her dark eyes twinkled. Suddenly, more than anything, Katie wanted to sit and talk with her mom. There were so many things she wanted to tell her and so many questions she wanted to ask about home and Dad and Michael.

13

Katie climbed the stairs, hugging all her birthday presents tight against her stomach: cell phone, notebook,
flashlight, Swiss Army knife and both new books.
At the top, she paused and stared down that long
gloomy hallway to Megan's room, wishing she had
somewhere else to go.

She drew a deep breath and trudged on slowly,
as if she were headed for the gallows. In front of
Megan's door she paused again. Hostility seeped
through the crack beneath it. Resentment trickled
out the keyhole.

Katie placed her hand on the doorknob. She reminded herself that already this summer she had
faced up to a furtive family of art thieves, two treach-
erous gold diggers and a couple of conniving land de-
velopers. And she had managed to survive. Why was
she so afraid of one faintly freaky teenaged cousin?

Besides, she glanced at her notebook and told herself, this could be a perfect opportunity to squeeze some information out of Megan. Her fingers tightened on the doorknob. Should she knock first?

Only if she valued her life. Katie tapped on the door and waited. When there was no answer, she took a shaky breath and inched open the door.

Megan lay on her bed, head propped on pillows, reading the book Katie's mom and Aunt Sarah gave her about birds of the prairies. While she read she raised her legs straight up from the bed, held them there, and slowly lowered them again. Emily's words filtered into Katie's thoughts..."They never stop exercising."

The purple lipstick and nail polish from Emily were tossed carelessly aside. Had Megan even thanked her? A tape recorder from Gram and GJ, for recording bird songs, sat on her desk. Who would have guessed that Megan was interested in birds and nature, just like Sheila?

Thinking of Sheila, Katie felt a pang of guilt. She had forgotten to phone and thank Sheila for the mystery novel. Tomorrow, she thought, tomorrow I'll phone.

She stopped abruptly. Lost in thought, she had wandered across the room and now stood much too close to Megan. So close she could see over Megan's flat stomach to the edge of a small, black, leather-bound book tucked against her side. "Do you keep a journal?" Katie asked, without thinking.

"What if I do?" Megan growled.

"Uh, I don't know, I just wondered..."

Megan scowled, but her eyes never left the book.

Now or never, Katie told herself. If she was going to question her cousin, first she needed to get through to her. So she straightened her shoulders, cleared her throat and began. "My friend would love your new book; she's into birds and stuff like that too."

Katie waited for a reaction. Still scowling, still raising and lowering her long thin legs, Megan kept her eyes on the book.

Katie started to back away, afraid to take her eyes off Megan. She had reached her cot when an idea popped into her head. It was the perfect way to approach her cousin. "Megan. I saw a couple of ducks today, in that slough up by the road. You know, by the poplar trees where Scott always parks his truck?"

Megan's head jerked up and she laid down her book, rested her legs. She studied Katie skeptically.

Katie swallowed. "So, anyway, they were hanging around that nest basket, and I kind of wondered what they were. Did you make it?"

"What?"

"The nest basket, did you make it? Because, if
you did, I think it's, like, really cool to do that, you
know, and help the ducks." And how come I'm, like,
talking like Emily? Katie wondered.

Megan's face softened. "What did they look
like?"

"Who?"

Her eyes rolled up into her brain. "The ducks?"

"Oh." Katie dumped her birthday presents on her
cot and gestured with her hands as she described
what she had seen.

Megan's scowl faded and her eyes lit up. "They
sound like pintails. I didn't realize they were there."

Megan's lips twitched. Katie wondered if she
might be smiling. Her cousin sat up cross-legged on
her bed and flipped through her bird book. She held
it open toward Katie. "Is this them?"

Katie moved closer. "Yep, that's them. Hmmm,
a male and a female." She drew a deep breath and
pressed on. "We found some chicken wire lying in
the grass too. Is that what you use to make the baskets? Did you make that one?"

Megan's face hardened. "I never meant to leave
it lying around!" she said fiercely. "I really thought
I picked it all up." She pressed her fingertips to her

forehead. "I don't understand what's happening to my brain."

Katie retreated to her cot again, wondering if Megan was thinking about the wire near the road or that other wire in the field. "It was an accident," she said.

"Of course it was an accident! Do you think I would trap my mother under the windrower on purpose?" Her voice rose to a shout. "I might be stupid and careless, but I'm not violent!" Her face crumpled and she pressed her fists against her forehead. "Haven't you figured that out yet Ms. Great Detective?"

"Amazing," Katie whispered.

"What?"

"It's Amazing Detective now, I've upgraded." Katie grinned to show she was joking, but Megan only stared at her, frowning as if she'd missed something important.

Katie felt the need to speak. "So, you dropped the chicken wire when you made the nest basket. Did you drop your cell phone by accident too?"

Megan went wild. She leapt to her feet, shouting, "Why does everyone say that? I told you, I didn't have my cell today! Someone took it."

Which led to one more question. But should she ask it? Would Megan charge across the room and quietly strangle her to death? Katie sidled closer to the door. "Do you think it was Scott?" she whispered.

Megan didn't charge. She stared for long seconds and then collapsed onto her bed. Facing the wall, she curled into a tight ball. When she spoke her voice was barely audible. "Of course not. How would he get in the house with all these people around? It has to be me. I must be losing it."

Katie settled on the edge of her cot, opened her notebook and started to write.

Is Megan right? Is she losing it?
What is "it"?
Did she have her cell phone tonight or not?
How did it end up by Scott's truck?
Three possibilities:

1. Scott sneaked in and snitched it when we were in Humboldt.

Why?

So he could use it to phone Aunt Margaret and blackmail her.

If he's behind all the accidents and phone calls, what might his motives be:

Revenge on Aunt Margaret?

Money for college—not much chance of that.

But why use Megan's cell?

Maybe the number wouldn't show up if Aunt Margaret hit call return.

He could phone from his truck and spy on the house at the same time.

He's trying to make Megan look guilty—don't ask why.

Problem with Scott theory:

Aunt Margaret locked the house up tight AND Cliff was here all day.

Megan must have been with Scott when that call was made, so she is either in on it, or,

2. Megan had the phone and lied about it (or forgot?)

Why?

Who knows? She does tons of dumb stuff.

Is she on drugs?

Problem with Megan theory:

Megan might be careless and forgetful and totally weird, but I don't think she's deceitful and dishonest.

Threatening her mom is miles different from doing dumb stuff by mistake.

The voice on the phone tonight was a man's, no way it could have been Megan.

So, if Megan took her own phone, she lent it to Scott to make the call.

Would they both be dumb enough to leave it lying on the grass where anyone could find it and check the outgoing calls?

Which leads to:

3. Cliff could have taken the phone when no one was home. He has a key.

He was outside when the call was made, so it could have been him just as easily as Scott.

Motives:

He wants a farm of his own.

He's trying to drive Aunt Margaret away.

He doesn't like Scott and wants to set him up.

How sneaky is that?

Problem with Cliff theory:

Why would he take Megan's phone?

If he's the one who made those other calls Aunt Margaret mentioned, why not use the same phone again?

Aunt Margaret says Cliff is such a nice guy. Is he really trying to set Scott up? Did he drop the phone out there on purpose for someone to find?

I must be missing something here.

Suddenly she remembered. She slid her hand into her short's pocket and pulled out the crumpled note.

Spreading it out on her notebook, she read it carefully. Then, since it didn't make one bit of sense to her, she copied exactly what Aunt Margaret had written:

GM canola
West field, near road
Call snitch line
Sued for all I own. Ha!

Katie thought for a moment, and then she added this line:

Tomorrow I need to question Aunt Margaret and Cliff. I need to find out...

A shadow flickered across the page. Katie shut her notebook and looked up. Megan loomed above her.

"What are you writing?"

"Nothing. It's just like, you know, a journal."

Megan's tongue clicked behind her front teeth. She pulled open the door and started out. Then she leaned back to peek around the door. Her lips twitched at the edges, and this time Katie was almost sure she was smiling. "You've been, like, talking to Emily too much."

The door closed quietly behind her.

14

"I'll help you with the dishes this morning, Aunt Margaret," Katie volunteered, hopping up from the table. She picked up her plate and reached for Rusty's.

He gave her a *What, are you nuts?* look and scurried out to the porch with his sketchbook securely under his arm.

"That's so nice of you." Aunt Margaret turned from the sink where she was running water for dishes.

Katie's mom looked surprised and suspicious at the same time. "That *is* nice." She picked up the nearest bowls. "I'll help too."

Katie almost dropped the plates. This was going all wrong. How could she question Aunt Margaret with her mom hanging around?

"No, Laura," Aunt Margaret said. "You've all been

working much too hard since you got here. Join the others on the porch and enjoy another cup of coffee."

Katie forced herself not to smile as her mom left the room. She put the plates next to the sink where Aunt Margaret was up to her elbows in soapy water. "How come you never use your dishwasher?"

"I would if I could, believe me. But it's so old it leaks like a sieve, and I can't afford a new one right now."

"I guess grain farms aren't doing so well these days." Katie picked up a dishtowel. This is good, she thought, she would ease gradually into the list of questions in her mind.

Aunt Margaret placed a cereal bowl in the dish rack. "Farmers have always struggled, Katie. We never know what the weather will do to us. Your Uncle Al and I had some good years though, when Megan was little. Then there were several summers when crops dried up in the fields. A few years back we had the best crop ever, and we were thrilled—until everything was destroyed by an early frost."

"But, if it's so hard, why keep doing it?" Katie asked.

"Your uncle and I thought about selling because so many big corporations are taking over farms.

They cultivate huge tracts of land using the latest, most expensive equipment money can buy and the fewest workers possible. It's almost impossible for family farms like ours to compete."

"So, why didn't you sell?"

Aunt Margaret rested her soapy hands on the edge of the sink and gazed out the window. Her eyes misted over. "Your uncle loved this land, just like Cliff does. Al always believed the next year would be better. 'Next year we'll be fine, Marg,' he would say every fall."

She picked up a plate and rubbed a gob of peanut butter from it. "Now I'm stuck with this farm."

"But, if Cliff loves farming so much, why not let him take over?"

"Trust me, if I could afford to, I would. Last year I considered selling out to a big corporation, or maybe leasing land to the Hutterites."

"Who are they?"

"The Hutterites? They're members of the Hutterian Church who moved to Canada seeking religious freedom. Most of them are farmers and they live and work together in large communities—so they can make a go of it where people like us can't."

"Then, why didn't you lease to them?"

"Cliff talked me out of it. He's sure, if we have a

good crop this year, he'll be able to buy from me next summer at a fair price. I promised I'd wait. He's been so good to us over the past two years."

"I don't get it." Katie dried another plate and piled it on the growing stack in front of her. "Why would Cliff have more money if you have a good crop? Isn't that your money?"

"Not exactly. We made an agreement. I can't pay him what he's worth, so he'll take a share of the profits this year."

"Okay," Katie said thoughtfully, "then that means he really wants the farm to do well."

"Of course he does!" Aunt Margaret put a plate in the dish rack. "But we've had so much bad luck lately, with the fire, and then a damaged cutter bar. Before that some cattle escaped and cost me a bundle. I only hope nothing else goes wrong."

"Do you think the accidents have anything to do with those phone calls?"

Aunt Margaret frowned. "Phone calls? Of course not. That's just some idiot playing a silly game. Threatening me for the fun of it. I guess they've got nothing better to do." She picked up the frying pan. "At least, that's what I thought until..." She broke off, madly scrubbing egg from the pan.

Katie dried the last plate and waited. Finally she

said, "Until that call last night? When he mentioned GM canola? What is it anyway?"

Aunt Margaret glanced up. "You are on top of things, aren't you? All right then, yes, that was the first time he mentioned GMO, and it scared me. GMO stands for Genetically Modified Organisms. Basically, it means scientists take a gene from one species and implant it in the DNA of another, to create a new organism. GM canola is genetically engineered, or modified, to be resistant to herbicides."

"Oh! You mean like superweeds?"

Aunt Margaret looked surprised. "Not exactly, although GM plants can behave like weeds. The pollen blows in the wind or is spread by insects; seeds are dropped by birds, or fly from passing trucks. Since GM canola looks like any other canola plant it can sprout up on your land without you even knowing it. If they spread into your wheat field though, or mix with other crops where you don't want them, they are very difficult to get rid of. Only the most toxic herbicides will touch them."

"So, you didn't plant any GM canola?"

"No. Even though Cliff thinks it's a good idea, I'm sticking to what Uncle Al and I decided. We thought GM crops hadn't been tested enough and might cause all sorts of problems in the future. By then it would be too late, and GM canola would be impossible to get rid of without killing everything else too."

"Wow, that is scary," Katie said. "Are you afraid GM plants will take over your farm? Is that why that phone call scared you?"

"As if that's not bad enough, my problem is even worse, Katie. You see, GM seeds are patented. That means I'd be in big trouble if any plants were found on my farm, since I didn't pay for the seeds. And this caller threatened to phone a snitch line."

"But that's not fair! If you didn't plant GM canola, it's not your fault."

Aunt Margaret sighed. "That doesn't seem to matter these days, which is why so many farmers are worried. All it takes is a rumor, and someone could show up to test your crops. No one ever knows what they might find."

"So, then that's what the threat is about," Katie mused. "Who do you think made it?"

Aunt Margaret kept scrubbing the frying pan, even though it looked perfectly clean to Katie. "I don't know. It could be someone hoping to pick up my land cheap, maybe an employee of a big corporation. Either that or it's simply someone out to scare me."

"Like Scott? Trying to get even for getting fired?"

"Maybe. I don't know. Sometimes I wonder if he

was innocent all along. That might explain why he's so angry."

"How could he be innocent? Didn't you find that necklace in Scott's room?"

"Yes." She handed the frying pan to Katie. "But Megan always liked that necklace. She used to wear it around the house sometimes. It was Megan who had cleaned the room before me. I just wonder..."

"You think Megan put it there to get Scott in trouble?"

Aunt Margaret shook her head. "Megan would never do that to Scott. But, what if she put the necklace on, just for fun? What if she was wearing it when she did the housework? It could have fallen off, and she didn't notice. I found it on the floor under the bed when I was vacuuming."

"That doesn't make sense. If it was Megan's fault she wouldn't have let you fire Scott."

Aunt Margaret's face sagged. She pressed her lips together and blinked back tears. She stared down at her hands immersed in greasy water.

"I don't know, Katie," she whispered. "I can't understand Megan lately. It's like she's in her own little world. She barely eats and she's always angry at everyone, especially me. I hoped that seeing you, so young and full of life, she might come to her senses."

Katie heard the clink of coffee cups being gathered together on the porch and rushed into her next question. "Do the calls ever come when Cliff or Megan are with you?"

"No, it's always in the evening when I'm alone. At least, I always was alone until you all arrived this week."

A peal of laughter was followed by soft footsteps. "Could it be Cliff?"

"What? Making threatening calls? No. Definitely not. He's the one person I can rely on."

"It looks like you two are out of dishes." Katie's mom came up behind them. "Never fear, I have more here." She laughed and put four coffee mugs in the sink.

A few minutes later GJ stepped into the kitchen. "How about I set to work finishing that rock planter out front?" he suggested. "It looks like you ran out of time for it."

"Oh, that was Megan's project," Aunt Margaret told him. "Since it's her job to clear the fields with the rock picker, she wanted to put the rocks to good use. She had visions of a flower garden and a bird-bath and I don't know what else to attract birds. But she lost interest after a few days."

"Looks to me that there's enough rocks to finish the section she started," GJ said. "I'll take Rusty and Sarah with me. They're looking for something to do together."

"Katie," her mom said, "Gram and I are going to weed the kitchen garden out back. Do you want to come and help us?"

Katie wondered if she had a choice. "Uh," she said, "maybe later, Mom. I want to write in my new notebook first. Besides I helped with all those dishes!"

"Thanks so much, all of you," Aunt Margaret said. "I'm off to the canola field; it's due for spraying. Cliff's busy trying to repair the cutter bar, and Megan needs to move the cattle to the west pasture and see to their water."

Grateful for some time to herself, Katie settled on the screened porch to make notes about her talk with Aunt Margaret. She checked back through earlier notes. So far—not so good. She still had no idea who to blame. It was beginning to look as if the accidents were only that. Accidents caused by Megan's carelessness. But the phone calls?

They could be from someone who works for a big company that wanted this land, like Aunt Margaret thinks.

They might be from Scott.

In spite of what Aunt Margaret said, Katie wasn't ready to cross Cliff off her list. If he wanted the land as badly as Aunt Margaret said, would he resort to any means to get it for himself?

No question about it, she needed to question him. Katie closed her notebook, slipped it under her arm and set off to find Cliff.

15

Beyond the equipment shed was another outbuilding, similar in size, with a steep metal roof and vertical siding. Until now, Katie had not paid much attention to it, but as she approached, she heard the quick sharp rap of metal on metal. There was no door on the driveway side, only a small high window. A well-worn path led through tall brown grasses along the sidewall.

Before setting out on the path, she stopped on the driveway and looked toward the front of the house where three figures were hard at work. GJ was on his knees, smoothing a layer of mortar around a volleyball-sized rock on the low wall. Rusty and his mom were piling rocks into a large gray wheelbarrow from a short stack on the front grass.

Katie tried to get Rusty's attention, willed him to look in her direction. He staggered under the weight of a large rock, took several wobbly steps and dropped it with a loud clanking thud that shook the wheelbarrow. Rusty brushed his hands against one another to rid them of dust and grabbed the handles. He put his head down, his baseball cap pulled low on his forehead to block the sun, and tried to lift the loaded wheelbarrow. He pushed. His feet made walking motions, his heels kicked out behind, one after the other, but he was going nowhere. His mom hurried over to help.

As much as Katie would like Rusty along as back up, she didn't dare wait. Cliff was alone right here and now, not out on a distant field where they wouldn't be able to find him. She walked boldly along the path to the far side of the building.

Facing a dirt roadway that led toward the fields was a wide-open garage door. In front of the door was yet another piece of farm equipment. A dark green, metal contraption, it had two fat knobby wheels near the back. At the front was a hitch, like the one on Gram and GJ's trailer, to attach it to a truck or tractor. Between the wheels was a kind of bin, like an oversized wheelbarrow bucket. In front of the bucket, low to the ground, was a wide row of metal teeth, like a gigantic comb. This comb, or fork-type thing, was attached to a reel and it looked like the long teeth were supposed to scoop up something from the ground. The reel would then turn to lift the load and dump it in the bucket. Katie had no idea what this machine was used for. There were so many different machines around here; no wonder Aunt Margaret had no money left over if she had to pay for all of them.

Katie stopped at the open door where the metallic clang of the hammer was so loud it hurt her ears. At first she didn't see Cliff, only his shadow on the far wall. A shadow hammer rose and fell in perfect time with each ear-splitting clang. She gripped her notebook a little more tightly and checked that her cell phone was safely tucked in her pocket; then she stepped into the workshop. She lingered for a moment near the door. Hot sun streamed in and landed on Cliff.

As if the shop weren't stifling already, Katie thought, Cliff was working in hot sunshine and his T-shirt was damp with sweat. Sweat poured down the side of his face, and his jaw was set in a grim line. She wondered why he didn't take the cutter bar outside and work in the shade of the building.

She took a few steps closer and stopped again when she realized it wasn't the cutter bar he was hammering on so furiously. It looked instead like a long thick bolt with a dark green head. The bolt was held in a vice while Cliff hit it with strong sharp blows of his sledgehammer.

"What are you doing?" she shouted. But he didn't hear, probably due to those fat orange sound protectors, like earmuffs, over his ears. She stepped so close he couldn't fail to see her.

Cliff jumped, the hammer poised above his head. "Are you nuts?" he yelled. "You don't sneak up on a man when he's working!"

"I didn't sneak. I just wanted to talk to you. Can I help it if you didn't see me?"

Slowly Cliff lowered the hammer. He slipped the ear protectors down around his neck.

"What are you doing?" Katie repeated. "I thought you were fixing the cutter bar."

"I am. At least I'm getting to that next. I had another little job to do first."

"What's that machine just outside the door?" she asked. "Is that what you're fixing?"

He looked at her as if she didn't have one scrap of brain in her entire head. "That's the rock picker. I need to check it over before your aunt uses it to finish clearing the field Megan started."

He put down the hammer and wiped his damp brow with the back of his hand. Then he grinned. "Your aunt figures if she gets more rocks today, your grandpa will be able to finish that rock wall while he's here. Kinda like getting two birds with one stone."

"Good idea," Katie agreed. Then she decided to get right down to business. "Can I ask you a couple of questions?"

Cliff smiled indulgently. "I hear you're a bit of a detective. Okay, two questions it is; then I need to get back to work."

"Do you think all the bad stuff that's happened is just by accident?"

"No. I said it before and I'll say it again. I think Scott's behind all of our problems."

"Why Scott?"

"I don't trust him; he's a sneaky character."

"But, why would he go to all that trouble?"

"I told you before. Revenge."

"But that doesn't make sense."

"Why not?" Cliff's face turned angry and he stepped toward Katie.

When she stepped back he smiled again, as if he suddenly realized he was frightening her. "Don't worry, little girl, I'm not going to hurt you. But you really should stay out of this. I have a feeling Scott can be dangerous if he doesn't get what he wants."

"Can I ask you just one more question?" she asked.

"Seems to me you've already asked more than two.

But if you'll get out of here and let me get back to work. Deal."

Katie nodded. "All right then. It's about Megan's cell phone. How do you think it got out there by the road?"

Cliff shrugged. "I don't know. Maybe she lent it to Scott and dropped it later, after he gave it back. That girl is getting more scatterbrained by the day."

"Why would she lend it to Scott?"

"Who knows? Maybe Scott said he needed to make a call—he's very inventive. Has anyone checked the outgoing calls?"

Katie nodded. "We did."

"We who? What did you find?"

"Rusty and me. But, all we found was a bunch of numbers."

"Not one to your aunt?"

Katie shrugged "I'm not sure, why?"

"I hope you didn't delete them."

She shook her head. This was going all wrong. She was supposed to ask the questions.

"Okay, time's up. You've passed your quota of questions." Cliff pulled his ear protectors up from his neck.

"Okay," she shouted, "thanks." She started for

the door. A phone rang. Realizing Cliff might not hear it, Katie glanced around.

"It's you," Cliff said, holding the protectors away from his ears. "Your pocket's ringing."

She grabbed her cell. "Hello?"

"Hey, is that like, Katie?"

"Yes."

"So, I'm thinking, I can pick you up at like, twelve. Scott will be at his house for lunch. Can you and Rusty come over then to, like, ask your questions?"

"Sure, thanks, Emily. I'll go tell Rusty."

After the call, with her cell in one hand and her notebook in the other, Katie started again for the door.

"What was that all about?" Cliff wanted to know.

"It was just Emily. She promised to take us out today."

"Out where?"

"Just around, kind of a sightseeing tour. Anyway, thanks for your help. I have to go now."

16

An old truck, the color of a prairie sky, turned off the dirt road, rattled along the short driveway and stopped in front of a long ranch-style house with wide windows facing the road. The truck engine coughed once and then chugged into silence.

Seated between Emily and Rusty, Katie looked out at the house and the tall teenaged boy who stepped onto the covered porch to meet them. He waved. "Hey, Em!"

Katie followed Rusty out the passenger side.

"Hi, Scott," Emily called as she slid down from the driver's seat. "These are, like, Megan's cousins, Katie and Rusty."

"Hi, kids," Scott said. "C'mon in." He led them down a short hallway to a large modern kitchen. They settled around a square kitchen table next to a sliding glass door. Beyond the door a field of grain rippled into the distance like ocean waves in a gentle breeze.

Scott opened the fridge and pulled out a plate with three thick sandwiches on it. "If you don't mind," he said, "I'll eat my lunch while we talk. My mom left them here for me." He poured himself a tall glass of milk.

Watching him, Katie realized how hungry she was. She licked her lips.

"You guys hungry?" Scott asked.

"No." Emily shook her head. "We won't share your lunch. You've been, like, working hard all morning. Milk would be good though, if you've got lots."

Scott chuckled. "Please! Drink milk! All of you. We've got more than we know what to do with already, and the cows just won't quit."

Emily went over to help him. She poured three glasses of milk while Scott opened a cookie tin and placed it on the table.

Minutes later, after wolfing down his first sandwich, Scott rested his forearms on the table and leaned toward Katie. "So, Em says you've got questions? What about? Is Megan in trouble? How can I help?"

"Whoa!" Rusty said. "You ask more questions than Katie!"

Katie shot him an angry look but Scott laughed.

He was kind of cute, Katie decided, with his wide dark eyes, straight brown eyebrows and his hair that was blond on top but dark where it was cut so short over his ears. He had a narrow friendly face and a smile that made his eyes crinkle.

"Aunt Margaret's in trouble," Katie said. "And I'm not sure what's wrong with Megan."

"Megs has her problems." Scott's tone implied he didn't want to discuss it. He glanced at his watch and picked up the second sandwich. "What do you want to know? I need to get back to work soon. Mom and Dad are in town for the day, and I've got tons of stuff that needs doing around here."

"Okay, I only have a few questions. First, do you know how Megan's cell phone ended up in the grass near the place you parked your truck last night?"

He swallowed. "No! Why would I? I didn't even know it was there." He glanced from Katie to Rusty. "So it was you guys who answered her cell last night?"

Katie nodded and made a quick note. "Cliff said you stole it from the house."

"What?" He had been about to drink some milk but thumped the glass down hard. "Why would I? If I took Megan's cell, why would I have phoned it? Why would I want it anyway?"

"Did Megan have it with her when she met you?"

He shook his head. "No. She forgot to clip it back on her belt after she recharged the battery. Megan forgets a lot of stuff these days."

Katie scribbled a quick note and glanced up at Scott. "What about the necklace?"

"Necklace?" His face flushed bright red. "I never took it. I never stole anything in my life! Besides, if I did take it, why would I be stupid enough to leave it under the bed where someone would be sure to find it?"

"That's what I wondered."

"Are we almost done?" Scott drained his glass and picked up his final sandwich.

"Uh, not quite. I wondered if you knew how that chicken wire got in the field?"

His shoulders slumped. "Megan thinks it's her fault. She likes making those nest baskets, you know? She's a volunteer for the Wildlife Federation. Ever since she was little, she made nest baskets with her dad. Anyhow, I helped her do some last spring, before I got fired, but Megan made that one by the hay field herself. She's always been careful to pick everything up before she leaves."

"What about the one near the place where you always park?"

"I only parked there once." He shrugged. "I didn't know there was a nest basket there. Megan must have done it."

Katie recognized the lie. "Didn't you park there two nights ago?" she asked. "Rusty and I saw you drive away."

Rusty nodded agreement. "We saw you up near the house too."

"Oh that." Scott rubbed his hand over the top of his head, making his blond hair stand up on end. "Yeah, okay, you got me. I was there. I couldn't get in touch with Megan. I even risked making her mom mad by phoning the house, but no one answered. So I wanted to make sure she was all right."

"Why wouldn't she be?"

"She told me she couldn't take it anymore. I was afraid she might run away."

"Run away?" Katie thought back to that day. Soon after they first arrived Cliff drove up with a fuming Megan and her bulging backpack. "I think maybe she did, run away, I mean. I think Cliff brought her back."

Scott scratched his head. "He keeps a close eye on her. She hates that."

Katie made another note. "One more question," she said. "Did you phone Aunt Margaret and tell her you knew she grew GM canola in her field?"

Scott jumped to his feet. He walked to the sliding door and stared out at the wide yellow field, his hands on his hips. "I haven't a clue what you're talking about. Mrs. Piercy would never have anything to do with GM seed."

"But you know about GM canola?"

"Of course, who doesn't? Cliff talked my parents into planting GM canola seed two years ago. He said it was the way of the future. He said we'd get two-thirds more yield per acre and cut down on herbicides at the same time."

"Was he right?"

Scott turned around. "Yes, for the first year. Last year the yield was down. Now we're using more and more herbicides because the weeds have become resistant." He shifted nervously from one foot to the other. "Your aunt thinks genetic engineering is dangerous. She says GM traits will spread to other crops and contaminate every farm in Saskatchewan."

"You mean, like superweeds?" Rusty asked.

Scott scowled. "Where'd you hear that?"

Rusty looked surprised, and Katie realized it was time to ask her most important question before Scott stopped answering altogether. "Did you know someone threatened to call a snitch line on Aunt Margaret?"

Scott turned pale. He sank onto his chair and his fingers twitched nervously over his last sandwich.

"What's the big deal about a snitch line?" Rusty asked.

"If GM plants are found on a farm that didn't buy the seed, farmers can be sued 'til they have nothing left but their socks." Scott grinned down at his big toe peeking out of his sock. "And they'll have holes in them."

Katie realized she had at least one more question, but Scott was looking restless. He'd gobbled his sandwich and checked his watch again. So she plunged right in. "You said Cliff talked your parents into trying GM canola. What's he got to do with them?"

"Cliff? He worked here for years. Mom and Dad liked him, and he worked really hard. He was saving his money to buy his own farm one day. But after they modernized our farm and bought an air seeder, they didn't need him anymore. Truth is, they couldn't afford to pay him and buy the new equipment at the same time. And I was old enough to do the job by then, so they let him go."

"Poor Cliff!"

"Yeah, but things worked out okay. He's been at the Piercy place ever since. He might even take over their farm one day, which would be good for all of them."

"How?"

"Well, Megan can't wait to get away. She'd love to go to university next year."

"Exactly," Emily spoke up. "Megan's wanted to be a wildlife biologist since, like, forever. And her mom is so, like, sick of the farm she's totally freaked out."

"If they had enough money, they'd be gone just like that." Scott snapped his fingers.

"Then," Rusty asked, "why don't they sell the farm to Cliff and move to Victoria? I mean, it's huge! It must be worth millions."

Scott and Emily shook their heads sadly.

"The thing is," Scott said, "even if they sold the house and every acre of the farm, they wouldn't have enough to buy a house in Victoria. Their machinery is too old to be worth much either. But still, Cliff doesn't have enough money to buy the land."

"Reality check," Emily said. "We're all stuck here forever, whether we like it or not."

"So how come Cliff wants to stay?" Rusty asked. "He's not stuck here."

"Cliff's one of those people who loves farming. It's in his blood. He figures he can rent out one section to a Hutterite colony and farm the rest himself. His parents sell farm equipment, so they'd help him out with that." Scott stood up abruptly. "I've got work to do."

"Okay, I just have one more question," Katie said. "If Cliff could rent to the Hutterites, why can't Aunt Margaret? She could rent out the whole farm and go wherever she wants."

It was Emily who answered. "She thought of that last year. She even talked to the farm manager at the nearest Hutterite colony. But she decided it wouldn't be fair to Cliff. He's helped them so much and he thinks he'll have enough money by next year, so she agreed to wait. Besides, this way Megan gets to finish school here."

"Is that what Megan wants?"

Emily sighed. "Who knows?"

17

"None of this makes any sense," Katie said on the drive back to the Piercy farm. "At first I thought Scott was behind the accidents, like Cliff says, because he wants to get revenge. Then I wondered if it was Cliff, but he doesn't have a motive. Finally I decided Megan caused all three accidents because each one happened in a place she had just been working. But Megan didn't make those phone calls, so now I'm back to Scott. What if he's trying to make Megan look guilty?"

Emily shook her head. "Scott would never do that to Megan. They've been friends for, like, forever."

"Maybe it was both of them," Rusty suggested. "Absent-minded Megan caused the accidents because, well, because her mind is absent. Scott made the phone calls because he's mad about getting fired and because Aunt Margaret won't let him see Megan anymore. I bet they're in cahoots."

Katie snorted. "Cahoots? That's a weird word!"

"I think it's a cool word. Look it up!"

"You'll never find cahoots in a dictionary."

"Trust me," Emily interrupted. "Megan and Scott aren't working some devious scheme together. Megs might have her problems, but I can't believe she'd leave chicken wire in the field or start a fire, even by mistake. She's been like, working on the farm all her life. And, as for the cows, she couldn't have left two gates open by mistake."

"So, you're thinking it's Scott?" Katie asked.

Emily turned to Katie, loosely holding the steering wheel. "You're missing something, Detective Katie. Scott would never hurt Megan's mom, even if she doesn't trust him. You don't know Scott like I do. He's, like, you know, one of the good guys."

"Maybe." Katie had to admit, she liked Scott too, even if she didn't know him very well. She did know, however, that sometimes the nice guys fool you. She bent over her notes, trying to sort things out.

Emily leaned sideways, as if to read Katie's notes. "Here's something to think about. If Cliff is such a nice guy, how come he tries to keep Megan away from her friends? If you ask me..."

A quick intake of breath and Emily slammed on the brakes. Katie catapulted toward the windshield.

She stared out at three solid-brown animals with sharp horns. Then the seatbelt yanked her back.

Emily wrenched on the steering wheel, and the truck skittered sideways. It lurched violently one way and then the other, threatening to flip right over. Katie was thrown hard against Emily; then she tossed violently against Rusty, jamming him against the door. She was jerked back and slammed against Emily again.

Then came the thud. Loud and sickening. A ton of metal against a ton of flesh. But it didn't end there. The air filled with a horrible moan of fear and pain, and the grinding, crunching shriek of metal folding against itself.

At last it stopped. Everything stopped. No movement. No sound. Only smell. The truck cab filled with the dry smell of dust and the stomach-churning stench of gas.

Everything was hazy, seen through a blanket of dust and smoke. "Rusty?" Katie said. "You okay?"

"Uh, yeah, I think so. We gotta get out of here."

Katie undid her seatbelt. "Emily?"

There was no answer.

"Emily!" Katie shouted. "We need to get out of the truck!"

But Emily was slumped over the wheel. Her arms

hung limply to each side. And then Katie saw the damage to the truck. On the driver's side, the engine hood had buckled and bent in toward the steering wheel. The driver's door was caved in so badly there was no way it would ever open again.

Panic made her heart pound. What should she do? What if the truck caught fire? She swallowed, undid Emily's seat belt, and pulled her toward the middle of the truck.

"Is she okay?" Rusty asked, his voice small and frightened.

"I think so. Can you get out? I need some room."

Rusty pushed open the door, tumbled outside and turned around to help. Katie slid toward the open door, easing Emily's limp body sideways on the seat. But she couldn't move the older girl any further.

"Take her shoulders," Katie said and slipped down to the floor.

Somewhere in the back of her mind Katie was amazed at how calm she felt at this moment. She did not want to spend another second inside this truck, but she could not leave Emily. So she set about doing what she had to do.

Rusty slipped his hands around Emily's arms and pulled gently while Katie tried to help by easing Emily's legs toward the door. Emily was small and slight; they should be able to move her easily. But they couldn't budge her.

"I think her leg's stuck," Katie said. She squeezed into the space below the steering wheel and reached for Emily's left foot somewhere beyond the brake pedal. She felt rather than saw it jammed between the bent metal door and the truck floor.

The smell in the cab was stronger now, a sickening stench of gas, oil and smoke.

What can I do? Katie wanted to scream, but she needed to stay calm. She took one deep breath, let it out, and an idea came to her. It had worked for her once, why not for Emily?

Katie fumbled to reach the laces of Emily's sneaker. She loosened them and worked Emily's foot out of her shoe. Then she wrapped both arms around Emily's legs. "Okay," she said, "let's get her out of here."

Between them they eased Emily's limp form out of the truck. They carried her along the road and laid her gently on the dry brown grass of the roadside. The ancient blue truck continued to belch out smoke. Churned-up dust settled over it like dirty snow. Two fat brown rear ends were disappearing at an amazing clip down the road. The third cow could not be seen.

Rusty looked one way and then the other on the straight, narrow, lonely road. "We need help," he said.

"My cell phone!" Katie checked her pocket. It was empty. She ran back to the truck and spotted her phone and notebook lying in the dirt near the truck's open door. She picked up the phone and ran back to join Rusty.

"You calling nine-one-one?" he asked.

"Yes. No. I don't know. We're so far from anything out here. I'm calling Aunt Margaret. She'll know what to do."

She pushed Redial, glad now that she hadn't phoned Sheila after ringing Aunt Margaret's number last night. The phone rang three times.

"Please pick up," Katie whispered.

The answering machine clicked on. Katie took two quick breaths, waiting to leave a message, wondering what to say. After the beep she yelled, "Help! Aunt Margaret, if you're there please answer!"

She was thinking what to say next, what to do, when she heard a click. "What's going on?" The grouchy voice was unmistakable.

Megan.

"Is Aunt Margaret there?" Katie demanded.

"Would I answer if Mother was here? So, this morning she tells me to make lunch for everyone, like

I have nothing better to do. Then, Mother doesn't bother to show up, and they grab all the food and take off, and I'm left with a disgusting mess to clean up."

Katie's thoughts whirled. She needed Aunt Margaret, needed someone else to take over; she didn't want to think anymore. The last thing she needed was her weird cousin ranting on about her troubles. Maybe she should hang up and call 911...

"So what's your big problem?" Megan asked.

Katie glanced at Emily, lying beside the road, Rusty sitting awkwardly beside her. "We hit a cow!"

"What?"

"A cow, in Emily's truck. She's hurt–bad!"

"The cow?"

"Huh?" Was Megan out of her mind? Then Katie realized that maybe she wasn't making much sense either. "No, not the cow. Well, yes, the cow too. But it's Emily! She's unconscious. And we don't know what to do!"

The silence seemed to last forever. Finally Megan said, "Where are you?"

"We're..." Katie bit her lip. Her heart pounded so fast and so loud in her ears it interfered with her brain. Where were they? Where were they? She took a deep breath and let it out slowly, forced herself to calm down, to speak clearly. "We had an accident with a cow. Emily's truck is smashed up. I think the cow's dead, and Emily is hurt. She needs help."

"But, where are you?" Megan yelled.

"I don't know!"

"Oh, come on!" Megan spat out the words. Then she paused to draw in a slow noisy breath. When she spoke again her voice sounded so calm Katie thought for a second that Aunt Margaret had taken over. "Okay then, tell me which way you went when you left here."

"Okay. Yes. I know. It's the road that goes to Scott's place."

There was a moment's hesitation, and then, "Good, I'll bring Mom's car. I'll be there in a few minutes. Stay with Emily. Try to keep calm for her sake...and, um, make sure she's warm enough."

Katie closed her phone. Her legs shook so violently she had to sit down.

They waited. One on each side of Emily, the two cousins sat at the edge of the road and waited. Time slowed down. They listened for the sound of an approaching car, but the entire world had gone silent.

Emily moaned softly. Her head twisted from side to side, but her eyes remained closed. She moaned again. "My leg," she whispered.

Katie leaned close. She placed a gentle hand on Emily's shoulder and felt her tremble beneath her fingertips. "You're okay," she said, trying to sound confident. "We called for help. Megan will be here in a minute." She looked down the road, stretching straight and empty to the horizon. Where was Megan?

"Listen," Rusty whispered.

So faint she wasn't sure at first whether it was only her imagination, Katie heard the wail of sirens. "Megan must have called nine-one-one," she said. The sound grew louder, closer, until Katie sat back on her heels, confident help would arrive in a matter of seconds.

Emily gave a soft gasp of pain and reached up blindly and grabbed Katie's hand. Emily's fingers, cold and clammy, wrapped tightly around Katie's hand. "Are you cold?" Katie asked, but Emily didn't answer, simply squeezed harder.

"How could she be cold?" Rusty asked. "It's burning hot out here!"

"Megan said to keep her warm. Rusty, I think there's a blanket covering the truck seat. Can you go get it?"

Rusty ran to the truck and returned with an old brown blanket that smelled of grease and smoke.

He laid it over Emily. Then he straightened and looked down the road. "Where'd they go?"

The sirens had stopped.

"Hey, wait! Here comes a car," Rusty said. "I think it's Aunt Margaret!"

Moments later the rusty little car skidded to a stop and Megan jumped out of the driver's side. She ran and dropped to her knees beside Emily. "Em," she cried, "I'm so sorry!"

Emily's eyes fluttered. "My leg hurts," she gasped through clenched teeth.

Cliff climbed out of the passenger side. He glanced down at Emily. "She'll be all right," he said. "The ambulance will be here soon." He continued toward the blue truck.

"I didn't call nine-one-one," Katie admitted.

"I did," Megan said, "before I went outside. But they were already on their way."

"That's impossible."

"No." Megan swallowed. "It's not."

Katie glanced sharply at her cousin, surprised to see her eyes brimming with tears.

"Emily will be all right," Katie said.

"It's not just Em. Something's wrong with Mom too. GJ called nine-one-one from the field. Then he phoned me right after you did. He's bringing her back to the house, and the ambulance stopped to pick her up first."

"What happened?"

"I think...I don't know. Something about the rock picker. They told me to come here and look after Emily."

Suddenly the air split open with a thunderous bang, so loud it hurt the ears and seemed to echo off the land itself. Cliff emerged from behind the truck, a rifle at his side. "It was one of our cows all right," he said.

Gently he took Megan's hand and raised her to her feet. "Don't worry. It wasn't your fault. I know you wouldn't have left the gates open again. Scott's behind this, just like he's behind everything else that's happened around here lately. He's driving your Mom crazy and making you look bad. It's high time I did something about it."

"No." Megan shook her head. "Scott would never hurt us. It's me. I mess up everything I touch! I was supposed to do the rock picking, not my mother! Everything that's happened is my fault! You should have let me leave when I wanted to!"

Cliff shook his head. "I'm not giving up on you, Megan. Don't you see? That's exactly what Scott wants. He hangs around, pretending to be your best friend. Then, when you're not looking, he stabs you in the back."

Tears streamed down Megan's face. "But why?" she whispered.

The sirens started up again. Minutes later a police car, followed closely by an ambulance, roared toward them. Behind the ambulance was their grandparents' shiny silver truck.

The sirens died as the police car slowed and crept past the kids to stop at Emily's shattered truck. When the ambulance pulled up near Emily, Megan ran toward it. "How's my mother?" she shouted. "I need to see her!"

Gram appeared quite suddenly, out of nowhere. She placed both hands on Megan's shoulders. "Megan," she soothed, "your mom's having some chest pains. Right now the paramedics are giving her oxygen." With an arm around Megan's shoulders, Gram led her toward their truck. "Come on, we'll take you to the hospital. You can see her there. Let the paramedics do their work, and I'm sure she'll be fine."

Katie sat on the roadside and watched everyone as if she were in a dream. A nightmare, she thought; her world had gone completely crazy. Emily, hurt, on a stretcher now, was being loaded into the ambulance.

Something wrong with Aunt Margaret. A cow dead. Police milling around Emily's truck, taking measurements, making marks on the dusty road. Cliff pulled one of the officers aside and spoke quietly to him. Katie strained to hear but managed only an occasional word such as "Scott," "threatening phone calls," and "dangerous."

Her stomach turned over. She should have figured things out by now. She should have done something to prevent all of this from happening. What kind of detective was she anyway? The answer was right there in front of her eyes, she was sure of it, but still she couldn't quite see it. You're missing something Detective Katie, Emily had told her less than a half hour ago. And Emily was right. But what? What was she missing?

Was Megan as forgetful and dangerous as she seemed?

Was Scott out to get revenge?

What was Cliff's role in all of this?

Katie's head spun. Her shoulder and stomach hurt where the seat belt had yanked her back. Her neck ached. She could not think clearly.

18

Katie ached from head to heels, and her eyes were so heavy she could barely keep them open. If she weren't so hungry she would crawl into bed right now. It was late evening. Katie and Rusty had been examined at the Humboldt hospital and released. Both were bruised and sore but otherwise fine. Now everyone was gathered around the table devouring a huge plate of sandwiches made by Katie's mom and Aunt Sarah.

Katie let her eyes wander around the table. Even though he looked as tired and sore as she felt, Rusty bit hungrily into a roast beef sandwich. Head down, Megan pulled a sandwich apart and nibbled on a piece of chicken. The adults were quietly preoccupied with drinking coffee and eating.

They had waited at the hospital for hours until Aunt Margaret was finally released. The doctors said she had suffered an anxiety attack, a serious condition that mimics the symptoms of a heart attack. And no wonder, thought Katie, with everything that had happened to her lately. It was enough to give anyone an anxiety attack.

Her face gray with exhaustion, Aunt Margaret looked even more worried than before. She used both hands to lift her coffee mug, but it shook so badly she couldn't drink and put it down again. "I thought I was having a heart attack," she whispered into the quiet room, "just like Al."

"What happened?" Katie asked. She spoke softly and tried not to turn her head because the slightest movement brought instant pain that started in her skull and shot down her neck into her right shoulder. So she held her sandwich in her left hand and took tiny bites because chewing made her face hurt.

"I was clearing a field of rocks," Aunt Margaret said. "I figured I'd collect a nice, big stack to keep GJ busy as long as possible." She looked fondly at her father. "When I had a full load, I backed the rock picker up to the truck and raised the bucket as high as it would go. Suddenly *wham!* The whole thing crashed down. Rocks, dirt, bucket, everything toppled toward the tractor. A huge rock bounced forward and smashed the window in front of my face. For a minute, I thought I'd been shot. Then a terrible pain began in my chest, so bad I doubled over and could hardly breathe. I don't know what happened after that."

"When Margaret didn't show up for lunch, we took lunch to her," GJ continued the story. "We found her slumped over the steering wheel."

"Well, it's over and done with now." Aunt Margaret smiled weakly. "And I'm none the worse for wear."

"That's not the way we see it," Katie's mom said. "Your doctor says you're ruining your health. You need a rest, Margaret."

"How can I rest? I have a farm to run."

"We talked it over while you were in Emergency. We're taking you home with us the day after tomorrow."

"I can't, Laura. I need to stay here and keep the farm going."

"The farm will be fine. Cliff offered to take over now, instead of waiting a year."

"And we have loads of room in our house," GJ said. "Your mother and I have been rattling around in it for years."

"If you won't do it for yourself, do it for Megan. She needs to get away from here," Gram said. "And she can finish school in Victoria."

Aunt Margaret glanced at Cliff. "No, I can't ask Cliff to do that; there are too many problems right now. The farm machinery is falling apart by the day, and there's that threat about GM canola I told you about. I need to deal with it."

"Don't you worry about that," Cliff said. "I can handle everything. You didn't want GM canola, and I respect your choice, even if I do believe it's the way of the future. Trust me, there wasn't one GM seed in the mix—not unless Scott put it there." His hand on the table formed a fist. "I know exactly who's behind the phone calls and I plan to take care of him."

"You still think it's Scott?"

"I know it's Scott. The police are questioning him right now. He's behind the accidents too. The RCMP helped me round up the cows and we found where the fence had been cut."

"When could Scott have done that?" Katie asked.

Cliff ignored her. "Scott must have sneaked onto the property after Megan last used the rock picker and damaged it before you used it today."

Katie cleared her throat. Before Cliff could speak again, she asked, "Is that what you were working on this morning in the shop?"

He looked at her and laughed. "What does a city

girl know about farm machines? You don't even know what a rock picker is. I was working on the cutter bar today."

"But..."

"If you do all this for us," Aunt Margaret said, "I'll need to sell you the farm at a drastically reduced price."

Cliff nodded. "I'm sure we'll reach an agreement when the time comes."

"But...," Katie said again. She tried to think through the pain that crashed inside her head.

"Do you have something else to say, Katie?" Cliff asked politely.

Did she? Something nagged at the back of her mind, but she couldn't quite remember what it was. She turned her head slightly and pain screamed through her body. "No," she whispered.

"I don't understand why Scott would do this to us," Aunt Margaret said.

"If you ask me, that boy's crazy. He's got a grudge against you and he'll do anything to get even. I knew we should have called the police when we caught him stealing your necklace."

"I guess you're right," Aunt Margaret agreed. "But I wanted to give him a second chance. He always seemed like such a nice boy."

"He's a good actor," Cliff said. "He has most people fooled, but he can't fool me."

Megan jumped to her feet and tossed her napkin on the table. "Don't you people get it?" she screamed. "It was me! I started the fire! I left the wire in the field! Maybe I didn't cut those fence wires, but I didn't bother to check the fence this morning and I almost killed my best friend!" She placed both hands against the sides of her head. "I must have wrecked the rock picker too. I forgot to tell you it wasn't working right the last time I used it. So, if anyone's crazy, it's me, not Scott!"

She ran from the room and charged up the stairs two at a time. Everyone sat in stunned silence, waiting for the inevitable slam of the door and the crash that would make the house shudder.

It never came.

"I'll tell you one thing," Rusty said into the silence. "This place isn't near as boring as I thought it would be."

To Katie's amazement, the adults burst into laughter. Even Aunt Margaret smiled, when only a moment ago she looked as if she would dissolve in tears.

Cliff grabbed a couple of sandwiches and stood up. "If you don't mind, I'll take these with me. I've got a ton of paperwork to do."

"What's all this paperwork Cliff does?" Katie asked after he left the room. "I thought he did repairs and farm-type jobs."

"Cliff volunteered to take over the accounts because he knows how much I hate doing that part of farm work. I was always stuck doing the books when Al was alive, but now Cliff does most of the ordering and pays all the bills. It's wonderful!"

"All the bills?" Katie asked. She knew this was important, although, at the moment, she couldn't remember why.

Aunt Margaret nodded.

"Do you think that's wise?" GJ asked. "I mean, are you sure he knows what he's doing? He seems awfully young to me."

"Are you kidding?" Rusty asked. "I bet Cliff's older than my fifth grade teacher, and he was ancient!"

"Right." Rusty's mom laughed. "He must have been at least twenty-five!"

"Cliff is only twenty-six," Aunt Margaret said, "but he's very competent. He went to Ag College."

"What's Ag College?" Rusty asked.

"It's where you study agriculture. Cliff knows all the latest techniques to get the most out of the land. He's also continuing the work Al started, to produce better canola seeds."

Something still nagged at Katie, something she'd been trying to sort out since this morning, but the accident had knocked it clear out of her consciousness. Now it kept creeping back, lingering at the edges of her mind, hazy and incomplete. She was so completely exhausted her brain seemed to be shutting down. Her eyes closed, her head drooped. "Can I go to bed now?"

"Do you want a nice hot bath first?" her mom asked. "It would soothe your aches and help you relax."

Katie considered. A hot bath would feel wonderful. "I don't have enough energy to relax," she said.

"You'll feel better after a good sleep." Her mom opened a tiny brown envelope. "Here, take this little pill. The doctor said to take one at bedtime."

Katie swallowed the pill with the last of her milk.

Her mom started to get up. "I'll come upstairs with you."

"No, Mom, I'll be fine." Katie got up slowly, stood for a moment to clear her head and then dragged herself to the stairs. She clung to the railing and raised one heavy foot to the first step. Then the other, one step at a time, until at last she reached the top. She walked down the hall to Megan's room. Pushed open the door. Sank in a heap on her cot.

"Where did you go with Emily?" Megan asked, her voice loud and abrupt.

"Huh?"

"You heard me. Where did you go in Emily's truck?"

"To see Scott," Katie whispered without opening her eyes.

"Why?"

"...solve case."

"So, you blame Scott too? Why can't you see it's me behind everything? Me and my stupid brain."

Katie forced her eyes to open. Forced her mind to focus. "You made those phone calls and threatened your mom?"

"What are you talking about? There was only one. On my birthday when I wasn't even home."

"Didn't your mom tell you about the other calls? Someone's been threatening her."

"Are you kidding? That must be why she had an anxiety attack! My mother keeps everything bad to herself. She thinks she needs to protect me."

The thought lurking in the back of Katie's mind became so clear she almost had it. She tried to focus; she needed to ask one more question. "Would your mom tell Cliff?"

"No way. She's always reminding me how hard he

works and how much he's done for us. She never
wants to bother him with any extra problems."
Megan lowered her voice and added, "Like, for in-
stance, me." In the faintest of whispers she said,
"Mom won't have me to worry about much longer.
There's no way I'm going to Victoria. She'll be better
off without me. So will Emily."

"But Emily will be fine. She just has a mild concus-
sion and a broken leg."

"Know what really sucks?" Megan continued. "I
was so rude to her. How could I treat my best friend
like that?"

Katie thought of Sheila and a sick feeling settled in
her stomach. "Phone Emily," she tried to say. "Don't
run away." But she wasn't sure if she said the words
out loud or simply thought them.

Everything was falling apart. Aunt Margaret was
about to give up. Megan was too. Katie tried to
think, tried to fit everything together, but that little pill her mother gave her was doing its job. She
drifted into sleep.

19

Katie awoke with a start. What was that sound? She lay with her eyes closed, listening, afraid Megan was already on her way, sneaking out before anyone else woke up. Then, from across the room, she heard Megan's soft breathing, in and out.

Tomorrow Megan and Aunt Margaret were supposed to fly to Victoria. But by then Megan wouldn't be here, Katie was sure of it, and while she might not miss Megan too much, Aunt Margaret would be devastated. So would Gram and GJ and the rest of the family. Which meant it was up to her to get to the truth. Today.

Her headache was gone and her entire body felt relaxed. She smiled and turned over in bed. It was time to do some serious thinking. Then she heard it again. The crunch of a footstep on gravel, so quiet she couldn't believe it woke her up. She opened her eyes. Deep purple curtains pulled back from the square of open window revealed the early morning sky, a washed-out shade of blue. The sound came again and Katie slipped out of bed. She padded to the open window.

Below her Cliff disappeared around the corner of the house, walking on the gravel path that led from his door around to the driveway. Katie looked longingly back at her bed. Her eyes shifted from the bed, back toward the window. They stopped in between, at Megan's desk.

Scattered across it were several books, a crumpled black T-shirt and Megan's new lipstick and nail polish. Her tape recorder sat on top of the bird book, with a little stack of tapes beside it. Katie studied the tape recorder, an idea forming in her mind. She glanced at Megan, but her cousin was turned away, facing the wall, and sleeping soundly.

Katie picked up the tape recorder, its book of instructions and two tapes. She dressed quickly in shorts and a T-shirt, grabbed her notebook, sneakers and some clean white socks and tiptoed from Megan's room. Soundlessly she made her way along the hall and down the stairs. She stopped at the office door and tapped softy.

There was no reply, so she pushed the door open

a few inches. Rusty had been sleeping down here since their mothers arrived. "Rusty!" she whispered through the crack. "You awake?"

Still no answer. She stepped into the room and closed the door behind her. Rusty lay curled on the loveseat, covered up to his shoulders in a light blanket, snoring peacefully.

Katie bent close to his ear. "Rusty! You awake?"

His body jerked. His eyes flew open.

"Rusty, I'm so glad you're awake. I need your help."

"Go away," Rusty moaned. He started to raise the blanket over his head.

Katie grabbed it and pulled, but Rusty hung on tight.

"I told you, I need your help. I'm going out to question Cliff, and you need to come with me. I think he's our man."

He looked up at her. "Why?"

"Wire cutters, phone bills and threats," she said.

Rusty let go of the blanket. "What?"

Katie smiled because she knew he was hooked. Rusty had a curious streak, just like she did. "I'll tell you on the way. Meet you in the kitchen."

The early morning sun shone in their eyes. Every little

pebble on the driveway cast a long, bullet-shaped shadow, pointed toward the house. The ping-ping-ping of metal tapping metal rang through the still air.

"Cliff sure starts work early." Rusty yawned.

"That's what farmers do."

"Gee, thanks for explaining. I never would have guessed." He yawned again. "I'm tired and my body aches from the roots of my hair right down to my toenails. So, are you planning on telling me why we're out here so early when I'd rather be sleeping?"

"Quit complaining, Rusty. I was in the accident too, remember? And I don't feel too wonderful either, but we have a job to do." She lowered her voice. "So, here's what I want you to do." They stopped beside the shop while Katie whispered every detail of her plan. Then they moved around to the front.

Cliff stood at his workbench, his back to the door. He picked up a wrench, turned and crouched beside the bright red harvest header that covered the cutter bar. He must have noticed Katie's long shadow flick across the cement floor because he stood up suddenly.

"Ah!" he said, "you again. You've got to stop sneaking up on me, Katie-girl. People can get hurt that way."

"I didn't sneak."

"What brings you out here so early in the morning? I thought you'd sleep until noon after the way you looked last night."

"I couldn't sleep. I heard you walk along the path and I needed to talk to you."

He rubbed a hand impatiently over his forehead. "Didn't we do that yesterday? I've got work to do here."

"I know, but it won't take long. There are a couple things that don't make sense anymore, so I thought you could help me figure them out."

Cliff smiled. "So, is our clever young detective unable to solve the case of who's behind all the accidents and threatening phone calls?" Then he frowned. "What do you mean they don't make sense anymore? What's changed since yesterday?"

"For starters, there were two more accidents: one with a cow and one with a rock picker. Also, I questioned Scott yesterday, and his story is way different from yours."

"That's no huge surprise. Did you expect him to admit he's been creeping around here, sabotaging equipment and endangering lives? I knew that kid was trouble even before he stole the necklace."

"Okay, but Scott said he never took the necklace.

He said, if he were a thief, he wouldn't be stupid enough to leave it in his room where Aunt Margaret would be sure to find it."

Cliff grunted and sat down on a high stool near his workbench. "All right, let's assume he didn't take it. Let's say it happened the way your aunt suggested and Megan accidentally dropped the necklace. That would mean he got fired for no reason. Don't you think he'd be mad enough to seek revenge?"

"Maybe." Katie nodded. "But Megan thinks everything's her fault. She says the fire, the wire in the field and the first escaped cows all happened because of her carelessness. Even Aunt Margaret's accident with the rock picker is her fault, Megan says."

"How could that be her fault? She wasn't anywhere near the rock picker."

"I know," Katie agreed. "Besides, you worked on it yesterday. Remember? You were hammering on that bolt when I talked to you."

"What are you talking about, Katie? Didn't we go through that last night?"

"Well, but that bolt...You had a dark green bolt, the same color as the rock picker. Is that what broke and made the bucket come crashing down?"

Cliff studied her for a moment, his forehead creased. Then he shook his head and smiled indulgently. "Of course not. Katie, you've got to understand how little you know about farming and the way we run things here. That's exactly the kind of thing I do. To save a few bucks and a trip into town, I took that bolt from an old piece of machinery. It was too long, so I had to adapt it to fit properly." He stood up. "And now, if you don't mind, I have work to finish before breakfast."

Katie glanced over her notes. "Did you cut the fence last night?" Her words hung in the warm morning air like daggers.

Cliff frowned. "What are you talking about?"

"The fence where the cows escaped. You said it had been cut."

"And you think I did it? Don't be ridiculous! Obviously Scott's behind it, just like everything else."

"When did he do it?"

"How would I know?"

"Well, it's odd, because when we saw you the night before, you said you checked the fence. Remember? And you had the wire cutters in your pocket."

Cliff looked frustrated. "Katie, I'd love to stand here and talk to you, but I need to get back to work." He turned away, dismissing her.

"But, I just can't figure it out."

Cliff swung around. "It's quite simple. He drove over in the morning, before you went to see him."

"Hmmm." Katie looked at her notes.

Cliff crouched beside the cutter bar and peered underneath it. He glanced up at Katie. "Are you finished yet?"

"Almost. I just wonder..."

"What?"

"Okay. Scott's parents took the truck into town early yesterday morning. So, I wonder how he got all the way here and back again in time to answer the phone when Emily called him?"

Cliff rubbed a hand over his damp forehead. "How would I know? Rode his bike? What difference does it make?"

Katie shrugged.

"Listen, Katie, it's been fun chatting with you and all, but I really have work to do now."

"No problem. I'll ask you the other stuff when you come in for breakfast." She turned to go.

"What other stuff?"

"Nothing important," she called over her shoulder. "It's only about the phone calls."

"What about them?"

She stopped in the wide doorway, with the sun at her back. She knew she was taking a chance now.

What if Megan was wrong and Aunt Margaret had told Cliff about the threatening calls? But things were not going well so far and it was a chance she needed to take. "Oh, you know, I just wondered how you knew about them when Aunt Margaret didn't tell anyone?"

"She told me. She must have. Why wouldn't she?" He scratched his head. "No, wait. I was there a couple of times when a call came in. I told her it must be Scott."

Katie made a point of reading through her notes. "Hmm," she said. "Interesting." She looked up at Cliff. "I have to go now, I need to talk to Aunt Margaret." She turned away.

"Wait! Katie!" Cliff moved swiftly toward her. "Maybe I can help. Have you got any more questions?"

Katie remained just inside the workshop door. "Well, okay. Maybe just one more. Remember when you said we should check Megan's cell phone because the last threatening call was made from it?"

Cliff looked wary. "Uh, did I say that?"

"Yeah, you did. So, I wondered how you knew?"

Before Katie could move he had covered the distance between them. He stood so close he was practically touching her, but not quite. The cow-smell of him filled her nostrils; she couldn't breathe properly; she wanted to run, but didn't dare move.

"Listen to me, Katie. These people trust me. Heck, they're even grateful to me. Nothing you say is going to change that, understand? You're just a kid, and it's your word against mine."

"But, why are you doing this? Can't you wait until next year to get the farm?"

"Not if I can take over now and buy it for half the price when the crops are sold. Your aunt can't sell the farm so long as there's the question of illegally planted GM seed hanging over her head. And right now she can't wait to get away from here."

"So you made up the whole GMO thing just to scare her?"

He grinned. "Devious, huh? The threats will disappear once Scott's out of the way."

"What about Megan?"

"Poor Megan is confused. She needed my help to realize that Scott isn't the right boy for her."

"Is that why you picked on Scott? Because Megan likes him?"

Cliff shrugged. "I got kicked off his parents' farm because of him. I couldn't let it happen again. Next thing I know he'll want a farm of his own."

"So...you're afraid Megan might marry Scott and take over this farm?"

"Not anymore." He chuckled. "And to think, I

once considered marrying that girl myself next year, but she turned out way too weird for my taste."

"Even Megan has more sense than to marry you! If she's weird it's because you made her think all the accidents were her fault!"

"Can I help it if accidents follow her around? She's always running off to meet Scott, and every time she does, something bad happens. Now she's not sure who she can trust."

"Was she going to see Scott the day we arrived?"

Cliff shook his head. "No. She decided to run away after she let that fire get out of control—or thought she did. Megan figures her mom would be better off without her. I brought her back, though. Margaret will never leave without her daughter."

Katie stared up at him in amazement. His plan was so clever she almost admired him. Blame Scott, make Megan feel so guilty she ruins her health, send her and Aunt Margaret away and get the farm for himself. "You're a sick man," she said.

He laughed. "And the best part of it is, no one knows but you and me."

"Who says I won't tell?"

"As I said, it's your word against mine. And just to be on the safe side," he glanced down at the wrench in his hand, "remember, accidents happen."

"I'm not afraid of you," she said.

"Maybe not." He smiled. "But you wouldn't want your aunt or, even worse, your mother to have an accident, would you?"

A chill spread over her skin. She had to get out of here. Now. Katie took a step backward. Outside, onto the dirt. She glanced to her left where Rusty stood waiting, out of Cliff's sight. But Cliff was so close, what if he followed her? Could they run fast enough to escape him?

"I'm going now," she said, hoping Rusty would take the hint and start moving away.

"And you'll keep your mouth shut?"

She nodded. "Yes, I promise. If you promise not to hurt anyone."

"Me?" he laughed. "I wouldn't hurt a fly."

She started to walk away, hoping Cliff would return to whatever he was doing.

Rusty hadn't moved. He must be waiting for her, to be sure she was safe. When Katie started toward him he nodded and pushed a button on the tape recorder. It beeped.

"Hey! What was that?" Cliff charged out the door.

Katie broke into a run.

Katie rounded the corner of the work shed on Rusty's heels. The thud-thud-thud of heavy feet followed close behind. "Run, Rusty!" she yelled.

"What do you think I'm doing?"

She caught up to him at the driveway. Which way to run? Could they make it to the house? Would anyone hear if they cried for help?

"Hey, kids!" Cliff's long shadow stretched across the dry dirt in front of them, one arm upraised, still clutching the wrench. "Stop, will you? I only want to talk to you."

If he caught them, Cliff would destroy the tape. Everything would be lost. "Keep going, Rusty," she gasped. "Run to the house, don't let him get the tape."

Rusty sprinted across the driveway. Katie made a quick sharp zigzag into Cliff's shadow. She dropped into a crouch with her chin tucked in to her knees, hands over the back of her neck.

Cliff's size and speed carried him smack into Katie's crouched form and sent him sprawling to the ground over her. The force knocked Katie down too, but she was ready for it and scrambled to her feet. She skirted around Cliff, who lay face first in the dirt, and headed for the screen door. But she wasn't quick enough. With lightning speed, Cliff's hand flew out and grabbed Katie's ankle, sending her flying.

Flat on her stomach on the dusty driveway, Katie tried to kick herself free. "You might as well give up," she shouted. "We know what you did!"

Cliff laughed. "Katie-girl, do you really think you're in a position to threaten me?"

"Rusty'll wake everyone up. He'll play the tape. Then see if anyone believes you."

"I don't think that's going to happen." Cliff tightened his grip, his fingers pressed into the soft spot behind her ankle bone.

"Ow!" Katie couldn't move. Dust filled her nostrils and made her eyes sting. "That hurts!"

"This isn't a game, girl."

Katie couldn't believe what she heard next.

"Thanks for coming back, son. Now, if you'll

just hand over that tape recorder I'll forget this ever happened."

"Okay," Rusty said, "let her go and I'll give it to you."

Katie twisted sideways to see Rusty standing over her. "What are you doing? I can take care of myself."

"That's not what I'm seeing," Rusty said.

Cliff released her ankle and stood up. Rusty handed over the tape recorder. "Thanks so much, Rusty. I knew you were a reasonable young man."

Katie sat up. "Did you at least call for help?"

"Of course I did!"

Cliff grinned as he removed the tape and slid it into his pocket. Then he handed the tape recorder back to Rusty. "It's a pleasure doing business with you."

"We'll tell them what you did," Katie threatened.

Cliff winked down at her. "As I said, it's your word against mine. Who do you think they'll believe? Kind and reliable Cliff, or a couple of light-fingered kids?" He walked away, chuckling.

Still sitting in the dirt, Katie watched him return to his workshop. They had been so close! Hot tears stung the backs of her eyes.

"Katie? Rusty? What's going on here?" Aunt Margaret

ran up to them, panting slightly, her face tight with concern. "I heard Rusty call for help. Are you all right, Katie?"

"I think so."

"Katie!" Cliff charged back from the workshop. "What happened? Are you hurt?"

He sounded so concerned Katie almost believed him. "I fell," she said and started to get up.

Rusty put out a hand to help. "It's okay," he whispered and tapped the tape recorder.

"But, why are you out here at this hour?" Aunt Margaret asked.

"I woke Rusty up early because I felt kind of sick in that hot stuffy bedroom. We came out to get some fresh air." She put her hand to her forehead. "I don't know what happened—all of a sudden I was lying on the driveway."

"It was weird," Rusty confirmed. "One minute she was walking along, then *KABOOM*, she crashed."

"That accident yesterday must have affected you more than we thought." Aunt Margaret wrapped a supportive arm around Katie's shoulders. "Let's get you inside."

As soon as they entered the kitchen, Cliff glanced sharply at Rusty. "What have you got there, young man?"

"Uh," Rusty stared down at his hands.

"Do you have a problem understanding what belongs to you?" Cliff reached for the tape recorder. "First you take Megan's cell phone and now her tape recorder?"

Rusty clutched the tape recorder and moved away. "No...I..." His eyes flicked to Katie.

She said the first thing that came to mind. "Megan said we could borrow it to record some early morning bird songs because she never gets up in time."

"And?" Aunt Margaret looked suspicious. "Did you get any?"

"Uh, I'm not sure. Want to listen and find out?"

"Sit down, Katie,"Aunt Margaret said. "I'll get you a glass of orange juice. You aren't looking so good. And Rusty, I think you'd better wake up Megan and the others. We need to get to the bottom of this."

"Leave the tape recorder with me," Cliff said, but Rusty ignored him and ran for the stairs.

Cliff started after him and then seemed to change his mind. Instead, he walked to the coffee machine, poured himself a mug and sat down next to Katie.

Katie sipped her juice and tried to ignore Cliff, but he was so close his sweaty barn-smell made that difficult. It seemed like forever before the entire family, including Megan, gathered in the kitchen.

"Now," Aunt Margaret said and turned to Megan, "it seems Katie and Rusty borrowed your tape recorder this morning. Is it true you asked them to record something for you?"

Megan yawned. She scowled first at Rusty and then at Katie. "Uh," she said, "like what?"

"So, you didn't say they could borrow it?" Cliff asked. He gave Aunt Sarah a sympathetic look. "I'm afraid your son is a kleptomaniac."

"A who?" Rusty asked.

"A kleptomaniac," Katie told him. "It means you steal stuff and you don't even know why."

"I never stole anything!"

"Son," Cliff said, "we caught you with Megan's cell phone two days ago, and now you have her tape recorder. How do you explain that?"

There was a long silence during which everyone looked at Rusty. His face quickly turned from pale white to bright red. "But, we recorded some interesting stuff," he said.

"Not birds though," Katie added. "I questioned Cliff this morning, and Rusty recorded it. You should hear what he said."

"This is ridiculous!" Cliff reached toward Rusty. "There isn't even a tape in there. Hand it over, son."

"How would you know that, Cliff?" Katie asked.

Cliff turned to her in surprise.

Megan's eyes moved slowly from Rusty to Cliff to Katie. "Uh," she rubbed her fingertips against her forehead, "I kinda forgot, maybe I did lend it to them. Why don't we listen to what they got?" She took the tape recorder from Rusty.

Cliff flashed a smile at her and held out his hand. "Give it to me."

But Megan turned away and took a close look at the tape recorder. "There's a tape in here, all right."

Cliff's smile faded. "It must be a blank."

"I don't think so." Rusty grinned.

"There's only one way to find out," Katie said.

Megan rewound the tape and pressed Play. There was a rustle of background noise and then Cliff's voice burst into the room, "Ah! It's you again. You've got to stop sneaking up on me, Katie-girl. People can get hurt that way."

"This is nuts!" Cliff shouted. "Are you really going to believe what these two kids say against me?" He appealed to Aunt Margaret, "After all I've done for you?"

"Shh," she said, "let's listen."

Around the table, they all stared at the tape recorder in complete silence until the final words:

"I'm going now," Katie's voice said.

"And you'll keep your mouth shut?" Cliff asked.

"Yes, I promise. If you promise not to hurt anyone."

"Me?" Cliff laughed. "I wouldn't hurt a fly."

Anger flashed in Aunt Margaret's eyes. She glared across the table at Cliff. "I trusted you," she said. "And all the time you were out to destroy us?"

He tried a smile, but it didn't flash as confidently as before. "No, I..."

"I thought it was me," Megan interrupted, leaping to her feet. "You told me every time I did something stupid, Mom got hurt. You told me my friends were a bad influence, but you would take care of me. You even kept track of my phone calls!" She raised her fists as if she would pummel Cliff on the shoulders, but then she backed away. "And all the time you were playing with my mind!"

"Look," Cliff stood up and moved toward Megan, "you don't understand."

Megan stood her ground. "You're wrong. I finally do understand. You made me think there was something wrong with me! You destroyed my life! And for what? To steal our farm from us!"

Aunt Margaret stood up then, and hurried to

place herself between Megan and Cliff. "I'll give you exactly fifteen minutes to clear out of here."

Cliff glared at her in fury. "You can't do this to me!" he shouted. "After all I've worked for!"

GJ got up abruptly. "Katie," he said, "use your cell phone and call the police. Now."

He strode angrily toward Cliff. "My daughter asked you to leave," he said. "You have your chance to walk away. Take off now, and they may not pick you up, but if any of us ever see your face around here again, I think the police will be interested in hearing that tape, don't you?"

Shaking with anger, Cliff pointed at Katie. "This is all your fault!"

"Yes," Katie said into her phone. "We need the police. Right now!"

Cliff turned and stomped from the room.

"And don't take anything that doesn't belong to you!" Aunt Margaret called after him.

Twenty minutes later, they stood on the porch watching Cliff walk up the driveway, carrying a large case.

"Are you going to let him walk away?" Katie asked.

"I just want him out of our lives," Aunt Margaret said.

"But, what if he does the same thing to someone

else? Besides, I told the nine-one-one operator he was dangerous."

Before Aunt Margaret could answer, they heard the scream of sirens; then they saw a white RCMP car race up the road. It stopped in front of Cliff. Both doors swung open and two officers stepped out.

Minutes later the police drove up to the house with Cliff in the backseat.

"You took five minutes too long," Aunt Margaret told him.

21

"You two did a good thing here today," GJ said soon after the police had taken Cliff away.

"We're proud of you," Katie's mom said. "And this time you didn't get yourselves into trouble. You played it smart."

Aunt Margaret turned from the stove, where she was ready to pour pancake batter onto a griddle. Beside her, Megan was slicing oranges for a fruit salad. "Without you two kids, we would have lost our farm and everything your Uncle Al and I, and Megan of course, worked so hard for."

"I told you we were good detectives," Katie said proudly.

She didn't realize until she saw Rusty's grin that she had included him.

"We're like traveling superheroes," he agreed.

"Or the Littlest Hobo and partner." Megan turned, smiling.

"Megan and I decided to take you up on your offer," Aunt Margaret said. "We're going to rent out the land and move to Victoria this fall, for Megan's final year at school."

"So, what do you think?" GJ looked at Katie's mom and Aunt Sarah. "Your mother and I plan to stay here for a few days longer. Then we'll continue on to Manitoba for a week or so, as planned, before returning here to help sort things out. Do you think these two can be trusted with us for a couple more weeks?"

"We can send them home by plane in plenty of time for school," Gram added.

"It's fine with me," Katie's mom said.

"Me too," Aunt Sarah agreed.

"Maybe someone should ask Katie and Rusty what they want?" Megan suggested.

"I'd like to stay," Katie said. "You never know who might need us next."

"Me too," Rusty added, "besides, we want to bond with our long-lost cousin."

Megan rolled her eyes, but for once she didn't scowl.

Dayle Campbell Gaetz is the author of three thrilling mysteries featuring her determined detectives: *Mystery From History*, an OLA Silver Birch nominee; *Barkerville Gold*; and the most recent, *Alberta Alibi*. Dayle lives in Campbell River, British Columbia.

Other books in this exciting series
by Dayle Campbell Gaetz

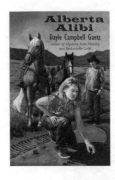

Alberta Alibi
1-55143-404-0

*Suddenly the air exploded. A gunshot. And it
came from behind them. Ben! Sheila stumbled,
half turned.*

"Keep going!" Wendell said.

*The air filled with another sound. Barking. At
the same moment a light flashed. On and off.*

Again.

On and off. The signal!

Other books in this exciting series
by Dayle Campbell Gaetz

Chocolate Lily Award nominee

Barkerville Gold
1-55143-306-0

"(*Barkerville Gold*)...fast-paced action...true historical details..." —*Resource Links*

Fresh from their adventures capturing daring art thieves in *Mystery from History*, Rusty, Katie and Sheila are back. This time the trio is in historic Barkerville, a gold-rush town abuzz with a story about a fortune in missing gold, a century-old curse and a missing miner. The friends find they are in a race against time to recover the gold and return it to its rightful owners to avert a tragedy. Will they find the gold in time? Or will they suffer the fate of Three Finger Evans, the missing miner?

Other books in this exciting series
by Dayle Campbell Gaetz

Silver Birch Award nominee

Mystery from History
1-55143-200-5

While exploring near an abandoned ocean-front mansion, Katie, Shiela and Rusty stumble across a long-buried mystery and a present-day crime. The trio of amateur detectives take on a case the local police department seems determined to ignore, and in the process, they put their own lives in the utmost danger.